Greek Billionaires

Two billionaire brothers...brides wanted!

Gorgeous Greek brothers Akis and
Vasso Giannopoulos have the world at their feet.

They have everything they need...except love.

Until their lives—and hearts!—are turned upside
down when two feisty women arrive on their
luxurious Greek island...

Akis meets his match—and the only woman who
can discover the man beneath the suit and tie—in
The Millionaire's True Worth

And

Vasso finds the woman of his dreams, but dare she
love him? Find out in
A Wedding for the Greek Tycoon

Let Rebecca Winters whisk you away with this
riveting and emotional new duet!

D1506713

Dear Reader,

Being a lover of the Greek myths, I came across the story of Castor and Pollux, two brothers who belonged to the golden age when mortals and immortals interacted. Their mortal, yet no less legendary, human family tree and history figure in some of the most ancient poems of the Greeks, such as Homer's epic *Iliad*. Though honored with temples and feast days, the deified youths lived somewhat less "heroic" lives than, say, Perseus or Hercules.

They did not, for example, take part in the Trojan War, nor did they emerge victorious from any daring feats. Their deification arises not from any wondrous achievement. Instead of heroism, *their fame lies in the bond of brotherhood*. This bond ultimately earns them their immortality. More important, it is what earns them a brotherhood that surpasses the ties of their blood relationship.

After reading about them, my mind conceived the idea of a Harlequin Romance duet about two unique brothers living in Greece who suffer and endure what some might describe as unheroic earthly trials to find their happiness. As such, their bond becomes greater than the whole of their blood relationship. The Giannopoulos brothers, Akis and Vasso, could indeed belong to the heroes of the golden age.

Enjoy!

Rebecca Winters

A Wedding for the Greek Tycoon

Rebecca Winters

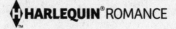

Recycling programs
for this product may
not exist in your area.

ISBN-13: 978-0-373-74353-7

A Wedding for the Greek Tycoon

First North American Publication 2015

Copyright © 2015 by Rebecca Winters

This edition published by arrangement with Harlequin Books S.A.

For questions and comments about the quality of this book, please contact us at CustomerService@Harlequin.com.

Printed in U.S.A.

www.Harlequin.com

Rebecca Winters lives in Salt Lake City, Utah. With canyons and high alpine meadows full of wildflowers, she never runs out of places to explore. They, plus her favorite vacation spots in Europe, often end up as backgrounds for her romance novels, because writing is her passion, along with her family and church.

Rebecca loves to hear from readers. If you wish to email her, please visit her website at cleanromances.com.

Books by Rebecca Winters

HARLEQUIN ROMANCE

Greek Billionaires

The Millionaire's True Worth

The Greek's Tiny Miracle
At the Chateau for Christmas
Taming the French Tycoon
The Renegade Billionaire

Visit the Author Profile page
at Harlequin.com for more titles.

To my wonderful grandsons, Billy and Jack.

These two brothers show a love and devotion
to each other that touches my heart.

CHAPTER ONE

August 9, New York City

THE BEARDED OLDER DOCTOR looked at Zoe. "Young woman. You've been cancer-free for eight months. Today I can say without reservation that it's definitely in remission. We've already talked about the life span for recovering patients like you. But no one can predict the end of life for any of us."

"I know," she said as he continued to explain the survival expectancy statistics for patients like her. But she'd read about it all before and didn't really listen. The adage to take it one day at a time and rejoice for another day of life was the motto around the hospital.

Zoe's physical exam had gone without incident. Her labs looked great. But she would never outgrow her nervousness. Fear lurked in her that the next time she had to have a checkup, the cancer would have come back. She couldn't throw it off.

The therapist at the center had given her a book to read about dealing with the disease once it had gone into remission. Depression bothered many patients who feared a recurrence and that was a problem they needed to deal with. Since Zoe was a prime example, she could have written that section of the book herself.

But for today she was filled with relief over the lab results. In fact she was so overjoyed with the news she had difficulty believing it. A year ago she'd been told she had a terminal case, but now… She looked at the doctor. "So what you're saying is—it's really gone."

His brows furrowed. "Believe it, girl."

She believed it for today, but it would come back.

"I'm pleased that the terrible fatigue you felt for so long is now gone. You seem much stronger physically and emotionally. Your therapist and I believe you're ready to leave the center today if you wish."

That was the news she'd been waiting for. She had plans and there was no time to lose.

"Here's hoping that from now on you can live a normal life."

Normal… It would never be normal when she knew the cancer would return. But she smiled at him. "How can I thank you for everything you've done for me?"

"You already have by working so hard to get well. You have a beautiful spirit and are an inspiration to the other patients here in the hospital. All the friends you've made here will miss you."

Tears stung her eyes. "I'll miss them more." With this checkup behind her, she could put her plan into action.

"I doubt that."

Zoe folded her arms to her waist. "My bill has to be astronomical. If it takes me the rest of my life, I'm going to pay back every cent of it."

"It's been taken care of by the generosity of the Giannopoulos Foundation Charity."

"I'm aware of that." So aware, in fact, she needed to thank the members of the Giannopoulos family personally and one day she would. "But everyone who works here is an angel, especially you. I don't know what I ever did to deserve such care."

When she'd been admitted to the hospital, she'd read the material given to every patient. The first time she'd gone to the chapel inside the hospital she'd read the plaque. It had been named for the Church of Agii Apostoli in Greece.

In honor of Patroklos Giannopoulos and his wife Irana Manos who survived the malaria outbreak on Paxos in the early 1960s.

In honor of her brother Kristos Manos who survived the malaria outbreak and emigrated to New York to build a new life.

In honor of Patroklos Giannopoulos who died from lymphoma.

"I'm here by the grace of the foundation here in New York too," the doctor reminded her. "It was established for Greek Americans with lymphoma who have no living family or means for the kind of help you've needed.

There are some wonderful, generous people in this world. Do you have a place to go?"

"Yes. Father Debakis at the Sacred Trinity Greek Orthodox Church has taken care of everything. I've known him since I was young. Throughout my ordeal he's been in constant contact with me. I owe him so much, and Iris Themis too. She's from the humanitarian council at Sacred Trinity and has arranged to take me to their homeless shelter where I can stay until I find a job and a place to live. All I have to do is phone her at her office."

"Splendid. As you know, you'll need another checkup in six weeks, either here or at another hospital depending on what's convenient. It will include a blood test and physical exam for lumps. But you can contact me at any time if you have concerns."

Zoe dreaded her next checkup, but she couldn't think about that right now. Instead she stood up to give him a hug. "Thank you for helping me get my life back. You'll never know what it means."

After she left his office, she hurried through the hospital and walked along the corridor that led to the convalescent center. She had a room on the second floor. Having lost her family, this had been her home for twelve months.

In the beginning, Zoe didn't dream that she'd ever leave this place alive. At first the man she'd been dating had called her often, but the technology company Chad worked for transferred him to Boston and the calls grew fewer and fewer. She understood, but it hurt her to the core. Even if he'd told her he was crazy about her, if he could leave at the darkest moment of her life, then she couldn't expect any man to accept her situation.

Though there were family friends from her old neighborhood who phoned her every so often, the inmates had become her choice friends. With all of them being Greek American, they shared stories of their family histories and had developed a camaraderie so strong she didn't want to leave them. It was here that her whole life had passed before her.

Once inside her room, she sat down on the side of the bed and phoned Iris. They planned to meet in front of the convalescent center in a half hour. One day Iris and the priest would receive their crowns in heaven.

Zoe had emerged from her illness wanting to help people the way they'd helped her. College could wait. If she could go to work for the Giannopoulos Foundation, that was what she wanted to do. Of necessity Zoe would have to approach Alexandra Kallistos, the woman who managed this center, but any experiences with her were unsettling. The other woman was standoffish. Whether that was her nature, or if she just didn't care for Zoe, she didn't know.

Earlier today when they'd passed each other in the hall, Ms. Kallistos hadn't even acknowledged her. Maybe it was because Zoe was taking up a bed someone else needed, but the therapist had insisted she still needed to be here. Because she'd lost her parents and required more time to heal mentally, the arrangements had been made for which Zoe would be eternally grateful.

Ms. Kallistos had an office at the hospital and was officially in charge. All the staff, doctors, nurses, therapists, lab workers, X-ray technicians, orderlies, kitchen help, volunteers and housekeeping people reported to her. She was a model of efficiency, but Zoe felt she lacked the bedside manner needed to make the inmates comfortable enough to confide in her.

Alexandra was a striking, brown-eyed, single Greek American woman probably in her early thirties. Her dark brown hair flounced around her shoulders. She wore fashionable clothes that made the most of her figure. But she seemed cold. Maybe that wasn't a fair judgment, but the thought of approaching her for a position made Zoe feel uneasy.

If there was a problem, maybe Father Debakis would have better luck in bringing up the subject of Zoe working here.

August 10, Athens, Greece

Vasso Giannopoulos was nearing the end of the audits on the Giannopoulos Complex in Athens, Greece he co-owned with Akis, his younger married brother, when he heard his private secretary buzz him. He'd been looking over the latest inventories from their convenience stores in Alexandroupolis.

"Yes, Kyria Spiros?"

"Ms. Kallistos is on the line from New York. She's calling from the hospital in New York, asking to speak to you or your brother. Do you want to take it, or shall I tell her you'll call her back later? I know you didn't want to be disturbed."

"No, no. You did the right thing." The Giannopoulos Hospital and Convalescent Center were located in Astoria. But why she would be calling when he was scheduled to meet with her tomorrow seemed odd. His head lifted. "I'll speak to her."

"Line two."

He picked up the phone. "Alexandra? This is Vasso."

"I'm sorry to bother you, Vasso. I thought I could catch you before you fly here. You're very kind to take my call."

"Not at all."

"Everyone knows that you and your brother established the Giannopoulos Greek American Lymphoma Center here in New York several years ago. This is the fourth time that I've been contacted by a major television network to devote a piece to your lives.

"The managing director of the network wants to send a crew here to film the facility and interview some of the staff. More importantly they want to interview you and your brother for the featured documentary. I told him I would pass this along to you. I know you've turned them down before, but since you'll be here tomorrow, would you be interested in setting up an appointment?"

Vasso didn't have to think. "Tell the man we're not interested."

"All right. When can I expect you to arrive?"

"By two at the latest. I appreciate the call. *Yassou.*" As he rang off, Akis walked in the office. "Hey, bro. I'm glad you're back. Alexandra just phoned. One of the networks in New York wants to do a documentary on us."

"Again?" Akis shook his head. "They never give up."

"Nope. I told her to tell them no."

"Good. How soon are you leaving for New York?"

"I'm ready to head out now. I plan to meet with some of our East Coast distributors early in the morning. Then I'll go over to the hospital and take a look at the books."

"While you do that, I'll finish up the rest of the inventories for the northern region. Raina will help. She's a genius with accounts. You won't have anything to worry about."

"How's her morning sickness?"

"It hardly ever bothers her now."

"Glad to hear it."

"Before you leave, I have a question." Akis eyed him with curiosity. "How did your evening go with Maris the other night?"

"So-so."

"That doesn't sound good. We were hoping she might be the one who brings an end to your bachelor existence."

"Afraid not. She's nice and interesting, but she's not the one." He patted Akis's shoulder. "See you in a couple of days."

Vasso hadn't been dating Maris that long, but already he knew he needed to end it with her. He didn't want to lead her on. But Akis's comment had hit a nerve. Both of them had been bachelors for a long time. Now that Akis was married, Vasso felt an emptiness in his life he'd never felt before. His brother was so happy these days with his new wife and a baby on the way, Vasso hardly recognized him.

August 12, New York City

"Vasso!"

"How are you, Alexandra?"

The manager got to her feet. "It's good to see you."

"I walked through the hospital and convalescent center first. Everything seems to be in perfect order. My congratulations for running an efficient center we can be proud of."

"Thank you. I know you're busy. If you want to go over the books in here, I can order lunch to be brought in."

"I've already eaten. Why don't I look at the figures while you're out to lunch? If I see anything wrong, we'll discuss it when you get back."

"All right. Before I leave, I wanted to tell you about a young woman who applied here for a job yesterday. I told her she didn't have the education or background necessary for the kind of work we do at the center.

"Later in the day I received a phone call from Father Debakis at the Sacred Trinity Church here in Astoria. He knows this woman and finds her a very capable person. He wanted to know if he could go to someone higher to arrange for an interview. I wrote the priest's number on my sticky note in case you want to deal with him."

"I'll take care of it now. Thanks for telling me."

"Then I'll leave and be back in an hour."

"Take your time." Vasso's curiosity had been aroused by the mention of the priest. As she reached the door he said, "I want you to know my brother and I are very pleased and grateful for the work you do to keep this center running so smoothly."

He heard a whispered thank-you before she left the office. Vasso phoned the number she'd left and asked to speak to Father Debakis. Then he sat back in the chair.

"It's an honor to speak with you, Kyrie Giannopoulos. I'm glad Ms. Kallistos passed my message along. Since I don't wish to waste your time, I'll come straight to the point." Vasso smiled. He liked brevity. "A very special twenty-four-year-old Greek American woman named Zoe Zachos here in Queens would like to work for your charity. I've taken it upon myself to approach you about it."

"I understand Ms. Kallistos had reservations about hiring her."

"When I spoke to her on Zoe's behalf, she said this young woman doesn't have the credentials and flatly refused to consider interviewing her for a position. I disagree strongly with her assessment and hoped to prevail on you to intercede in this matter."

Vasso and Akis had flown to New York ten months ago to find a new manager after the old one had to give it up due to ill health. Alexandra had come to them with outstanding references and was the most qualified of all the applicants because she'd had experience working in hospital administration.

Akis, who'd been in business with Vasso from childhood, had flown to New York five months later to check on her. So far neither he nor Vasso had a problem with the way she'd been doing her work. She must have had good reason not to take the other person's application.

"Obviously this is important to you."

"Very." Vasso blinked in surprise at the priest's sobriety. "Perhaps she could be interviewed by you?"

He sat forward. "That isn't our normal procedure."

"Ah…" The disappointment in the priest's voice wasn't lost on Vasso, who'd been taught by his deceased father to revere a priest.

His black brows furrowed. "May I ask why you have such strong reasons for making this call?"

"It's a matter of some urgency."

The hairs lifted on the back of Vasso's neck. After the priest put it that way, Vasso didn't feel he could refuse him. "Tell me about her background."

"I think it would be better for you to discover that information yourself."

At this point Vasso was more than a little intrigued. In all honesty he found himself curious about the unusual request. "How soon could she be at Ms. Kallistos's office?"

"Within two hours."

"Then I'll be expecting her."

"Bless you, my son." The priest clicked off while a perplexed Vasso still held the phone in his hand. For the next hour and a half he pored over the books. When Alexandra returned, he told her everything looked in order and listened to some of her suggestions to do with the running of the hospital.

During their conversation, a polite knock sounded on the closed door. He turned to Alexandra. "That would be Zoe Zachos. If you'll give us a half hour please."

After a discernible hesitation she said, "Of course." She showed remarkable poise by not questioning him about it. He watched her get up and open the door. "Come in, Zoe," she said to the blonde woman before she left them alone.

Zoe? That meant Alexandra knew her.

Vasso didn't know exactly what to expect other than he'd been told she was twenty-four years old. He got to his feet as the young woman came into the office.

"Kyrie Giannopoulos?" she said, sounding the slightest bit breathless. "I'm Zoe Zachos. I can't believe it, but somehow Father Debakis made this meeting possible." In an instant a smile broke out on her lovely face. "You have no idea how grateful I am to meet you at last."

Tears had caused her translucent green eyes to shimmer.

When she extended her hand to shake his across the desk, he saw a look of such genuine gratitude reflected in those depths, it reached places inside him he didn't know were there.

"Please, Thespinis Zachos. Sit down."

Her lissome figure subsided in one of the

chairs opposite the desk. She was wearing a print blouse and khaki skirt, drawing his attention to her shapely body and legs below the hem. She had to be five-six or five-seven.

"I'm sure he told you that I'd like to work for your foundation."

He felt an earnestness—a sweetness—coming from her that caught him off guard. "He made that clear."

She clasped her hands. "When he spoke on my behalf with Ms. Kallistos, she said I didn't have the kind of background she was looking for."

"But Father Debakis feels that you do. Tell me about yourself. Why would you want to work for the foundation as opposed to somewhere else, or do another type of work entirely?"

"He didn't tell you?" She looked surprised.

"No. He's a man of few words."

"But he makes them count," she said with a smile that told him she'd had a running relationship with the priest.

Vasso agreed with her assessment. The priest had an amazing way of making his point. It had gotten Vasso to conduct this interview, which was out of the ordinary. "Why not start at the beginning, *thespinis*?"

She nodded. "I've been a patient here with non-Hodgkins lymphoma for the last year and was just released on the ninth of this month."

A patient...

Knowing what that meant, he swallowed hard. Vasso had thought of several reasons for the possible conflict between the two women. He thought back to a year ago when another manager had to resign because of health issues. When they'd hired Alexandra, Zoe Zachos had already been a patient here. The two had seen each other coming and going for months. But it didn't explain the problem that caused Alexandra to turn down Zoe's request.

"I was thrilled to be told I was cured."

The joy in her countenance was something Vasso would never be able to describe adequately. "That's wonderful news," he said in a thick-toned voice.

"Isn't it?" She leaned forward with a light in those marvelous green eyes. "It's all because of your family. The foundation you established literally gave me back my life!" The tremor in her voice resonated inside him.

He had to clear his throat. "To hear your testimonial is very gratifying, Thespinis Zachos."

"There's no way to pay you back monetarily. But I would love to work for you in some capacity for the rest of my life. I'm a good cook and could work in the hospital kitchen, or in the laundry, or give assistance to those convalescing. Give me a job and I'll do it to the best of my ability. The trouble is Ms. Kallistos told Father Debakis that without a college degree and no experience in the health field, there was no point in interviewing me.

"She wondered if I might not be better suited to becoming a nun if I wanted to be of service to others." A *nun*? "I'm sure she was just teasing. Father Debakis and I laughed over that. I'm hardly nun material. But I do want to make a difference."

Vasso's anger flared. Not so much at Alexandra as at himself and Akis. At the time they hired her, both he and Akis had decided she had the best credentials for the important position even if she was younger. But

Vasso could see there was a great deal more to finding the right person for this particular job than what was put on paper. Since Zoe had been a patient here for such a long time, surely Alexandra could have shown a little more understanding.

"Whatever was said, you have a great advocate in Father Debakis. How did you come to know him?"

"My parents owned a Greek *taverna* and we lived in the apartment above it here in Astoria near the Sacred Trinity Church. Father Debakis was serving there when I was just a young girl and always took an interest in our family. If it hadn't been for him, I'm not sure I'd be alive today."

"Why do you say that?"

An expression of unspeakable sorrow brought shadows to her classic features, changing her demeanor. "A year ago I'd gone to a movie with some friends from the neighborhood. We walked home after it was over. It was late. My parents would have been in bed."

She paused before saying, "When we got there, it looked like a war zone. Someone said there'd been an explosion. I ran towards the fire chief who told me an arsonist had planted a bomb in the back of the laundry next door to my parents' *taverna* where I sometimes helped out part-time. Fire spread to the *taverna*'s kitchen. Everything went up in smoke. My parents died. So did the owners next door who'd run the laundry for many years."

"Dear Lord." Vasso couldn't fathom it.

"Everything burned. Family photos, precious possessions, clothes—all was gone. I've always lived with my parents and worked in the restaurant kitchen to save money while I went to college. The scene was so horrific, I collapsed. When I came to, I was in the ER at the local hospital. Father Debakis was the first person I saw when I woke up.

"He told me the doctor had examined me and had discovered a lump in my neck." Vasso saw her shudder. It brought out a protective instinct in him he hadn't felt since he and Akis were on their own after their father died. Though Akis was only eleven months younger, their dying father had charged Vasso to look after his younger brother.

"Honestly, I'm still surprised I didn't die that night. I wanted to. I was convinced my life was over. He, along with Iris Themis, one of the women on the church humanitarian council, wouldn't let me give up.

"They are wonderful people who did everything to help me physically and spiritually in order to deal with my grief. The diagnosis of cancer added another level of despair. My parents and I had never taken a handout from anyone. For them to shower me with clothes and toiletries lost in the fire besides being there for comfort, meant I felt overwhelmed with their generosity."

Vasso got up from the chair, unable to remain seated. Father Debakis had told him she was a very special young woman.

"Before the fire and my illness, I'd planned to finish my last semester of college to get my English degree. I'd even thought of going on to get a secondary school teaching certificate. Because I had to work at night and go to school during the day, my education had to be strung out."

A sad laugh escaped her lips. "At twenty-four I would have been one of the oldest college graduates around, but the enormity of losing my parents this last year along with the lymphoma has changed my focus."

"It would change anyone's." When Vasso's

father had died of the disease, the world he and Akis had grown up in was changed for all time. They'd adored their father who was too poor to get the medical treatment needed. As he slipped away from them, they'd vowed never to feel that helpless again.

He watched as she re-crossed her elegant legs. "While I was still at the hospital, I met with a cancer specialist who discussed my illness with me. My student insurance would only cover a portion of the costs. There was only a little money from my parents' savings to add to the amount owing.

"With their insurance I was able to pay off my student loan. What I had left was the small savings in my bank account that wouldn't keep me alive more than a couple of months. I was trapped in a black abyss when Father Debakis and Iris came to get me and bring me here.

"I was told the center existed to help Greek Americans with lymphoma who had few sources of income to cover the bulk of the expense. They took me into the chapel where I read what was written on the plaque."

As she looked up at Vasso, tears trickled down her flushed cheeks. "At that moment

I knew the Giannopoulos family truly were Samaritans. You just don't know how grateful I am." The words continued to pour out of her. "As long as I'm granted life, I want to give back a little of what your foundation has done for me. It would be a privilege to work for you and your family in any capacity."

As long as I'm granted life.

What had Father Debakis said? It was a matter of some urgency.

Zoe Zachos's revelations had left Vasso stunned and touched to the soul. He sucked in his breath. "Are you in a relationship with anyone?"

"I had a boyfriend named Chad. But he got a job offer in Boston around the time of the fire. I urged him to take it and he did. We've both moved on. So to answer your question, no, there is no special person in my life."

Good grief. What kind of a man would desert her in her darkest hour?

"Where do you live right now?"

"I'm at the church's shelter. I'm planning to find an apartment, but I hoped that if I could work at the center here, then I would look for a place close by."

"Do you have transportation?"

"Yes."

"And a phone?"

"Yes." She drew it from her purse. "Iris will pick me up here as soon as I call her."

He pulled out his cell. "Let's exchange phone numbers." After that was done he said, "Before the day is out you'll be hearing from me."

She got to her feet. "Thank you for giving me this opportunity to talk to you. No matter what you decide, I'm thankful I was able to meet one of the Giannopoulos family and thank you personally. God bless all of you."

All two of us, he mused mournfully. *Four* when he included Raina and the baby that was on the way.

After she left the office, Vasso went back to the desk and sat down to phone Akis. He checked the time. Ten o'clock in Athens. His brother wouldn't have gone to bed yet. He picked up on the third ring.

"Vasso? Raina and I were hoping we'd hear from you before it got too late. How do things look at the center?"

He closed his eyes tightly. "Alexandra has everything under control. But something else has come up. You're not going to believe what I have to tell you." For the next few minutes he unloaded on his brother, telling him everything.

"When we created the foundation, it felt good. It was a way to honor *Papa*." In a shaken voice he said, "But one look in her eyes taught me what gratitude really looks like—you know, deep down to the soul. I've never been so humbled in my life."

"That's a very moving story," Akis responded in a serious tone. "What do you think we should do? Since Alexandra has made her opinion obvious for whatever reason, I don't think it would work to create a position for Thespinis Zachos under the same roof."

"I'm way ahead of you. What do you think if we hired her to work at the center on Paxos?"

He could hear his brother's mind ticking away. "Do you think she'd be willing to relocate to Greece?"

"I don't know. She has no family in New York, but she's very close to Father Debakis and one of the women working for the Church's humanitarian program."

"What about a boyfriend?"

"Not at the moment. But I'm sure she has friends she met at college. There was the mention of friends she'd been out with the night of the fire."

"She's definitely one of the survivors of this world. What does she look like?"

How to describe Zoe Zachos…? "I can't explain because I wouldn't do her justice."

"That beautiful, huh?" Akis knew him too well. After a pause, "Are you thinking of asking her if she'd like to move to Paxos?"

It was all he'd been thinking about since she'd left the office.

"Just be careful, Vasso. I know you inside and out. If she does take you up on your offer of a job, you're going to feel responsible for her. Be sure that's what you want."

He lowered his head. Funny how circumstances had changed. Vasso used to be the one watching out for Akis. Now his little brother had taken over that role. It gave him a lot to think about, but there wasn't time if he expected to phone her before nightfall. "I'll consider what you've said. *Yassou.*"

On his way out of the office, Alexandra was just coming in. "You're finished?"

"That's right."

She looked surprised. "Are you staying in New York tonight?"

"No. I'm flying back to Athens." The beauty of owning a private jet meant he could sleep at night and arrive where he needed to be the next morning.

"I see. What have you decided about Ms. Zachos?"

"You were right. Her skills can best be used elsewhere." Her bilingual abilities in English and Greek played only a tiny part of what she could bring to the job. "That's what I'll tell Father Debakis. Keep up the good work, Alexandra. My brother and I are relying on you."

Relief broke out on her face. "Thank you. I hope the next time you come you'll arrange to stay longer."

Vasso nodded before leaving the center. After he got in the limo, he phoned the priest.

"Father? This is Vasso Giannopoulos. I've just come from the center and am pressed for time. Could I meet with you and Thespinis Zachos in your office ASAP?"

"That can be arranged. I'll ask Kyria Themis to bring her immediately."

"Excellent. In lieu of her parents who died

in the fire, I look to you as someone who has her deepest interest at heart. I understand she has revered you from childhood. What I'd like to do is present an employment offer to her. I believe it's vital that you are there so she can discuss it with you." He paused, then said, "She regards you as her mentor."

"She's so grateful to everyone who helped her; her dearest wish is to work for your foundation. She lost everything. Now that she has survived, she wants to give back what she can."

"After talking to her, I believe that's true. I'll see you soon."

He hung up and asked the limo driver to take him to the Greek Orthodox Church a few blocks away.

CHAPTER TWO

ZOE DIDN'T KNOW what the meeting with the priest was all about. The incredible-looking man she'd met at the hospital earlier had told her he'd phone her before the day was out. Since leaving that office, she'd wondered if he'd really meant what he'd said.

But any concern in that department vanished the second she caught a glimpse of his black hair through the opening of the study door. Her pulse quickened for no good reason the second a pair of jet-black eyes beneath black brows zeroed in on her.

Both men stood when she walked in wearing the same skirt and blouse she'd worn earlier. She only had three or four outfits because no more was necessary living at the hospital. But now she needed to do some shopping for a wardrobe with the money she still had left in her bank account.

Over the years Zoe had been in the priest's study many times with other people, but she'd never laid eyes on any man as gorgeous as Vasso Giannopoulos. The thirtyish-looking male possessed facial features and a hard-muscled body that were as perfectly formed as her favorite statue of Apollo she'd only seen in pictures. No other man could possibly compare.

Her first meeting with him had been so important, she hadn't had the luxury of studying him the way she could now. He was probably six foot two and topped the priest by several inches, having an authority about him not even Father Debakis possessed. The dark gray suit toned with a lighter gray shirt gave him a rare aura of sophistication.

"Come in and sit down, Zoe. Kyrie Giannopoulos requested that I be in on this visit with you."

"Thank you." She found an upholstered chair next to the couch where he sat.

Father Debakis took his place behind the desk. He nodded to the younger man. "Go ahead and tell her why you've asked for this meeting."

Vasso sat forward to look at her with his hands resting on his thighs. Her gaze darted to his hands. He wore no rings. "After you left the hospital, I phoned my brother to tell him about you and your situation. We would be very happy to have you come to work for the foundation, but the position we're offering would be on the island of Paxos in Greece."

Zoe decided she had to be dreaming.

"Have you ever been there?"

She shook her head. "No, though I did go on a two-week university tour to England right before the fire broke out. As for our family, we took trips up and down the East Coast and into French Canada."

After a quick breath she said, "My great-grandparents left Florina in Macedonia to escape communism after the Greek Civil War and came to the US in 1946. It was in New York my father met my mother whose family were also refugees. They'd planned to take us on a trip back there for my graduation present, but it didn't happen."

"Maybe now it can," he said. "The center here in New York is fully staffed, and it might be a long time before there's a vacancy. But our center on Paxos has needed an assistant to the manager since the last one left to take care of a sick parent."

Zoe could feel her pulse racing. "You've established another hospital?" That meant she wouldn't have to work under Ms. Kallistos?

"Our first one actually. My brother and I have interviewed a number of applicants, but the manager hasn't felt he could work with any of them."

He? "What makes you think he would feel differently about me?"

"I have a feeling he'll welcome you because you have one credential no one else has possessed to date. It's more important than any college degree."

Her heart was pounding too hard. "What's that?"

"Compassion. You've lived through the agony of having been diagnosed with lymphoma, being treated for it and beating it. The year you've spent in the center here has given you the most valuable knowledge of what it's like to know you have the disease, and to have survived."

"Still, Ms. Kallistos said—"

"Let me finish," he cut her off, not unkindly. "For that kind of learning experience, you've paid a terrible price. Yet it's that very knowledge that's needed to work with patients because you conquered the disease. Everyone in the hospital will relate to you and your presence alone will give them hope."

"She does that at the hospital every day," the priest inserted.

Her throat swelled with emotion. "What's the manager like?"

"Yiannis Megalos served as a rear admiral in the Greek Navy before his retirement."

A man who'd been an admiral. How interesting. "Then he must run a very tight ship."

The smile he flashed turned her heart over. "He's an old family friend and came to us about a position with the foundation after losing his wife to cancer, in order to work through his grief. In that respect you and he already share something vital in common by having a burning desire to help. I don't need to tell you his organizational skills and his work with the wounded during his military career made him an excellent choice."

"He sounds remarkable."

"Yiannis is a character too," he added on a lighter note. She felt his eyes travel over her. "If I have any concerns, it's for you. Leaving New York to live in a new country is a huge decision to make. If you've got anyone special you don't want to leave, that could prove difficult."

She shook her head. "There's no one."

"Even so, you may not feel that you can uproot yourself from friends. It might be hard to leave those here at the church who've helped you. That's why I wanted Father Debakis to be here in case you want to discuss this with him in private."

"Of course I'll miss everyone, but to be given a chance to work for your foundation means more to me than anything."

"We can come to terms over a salary you'll feel good about. You'll need a place to live. But all of those matters can be discussed once you've determined that you want this position. Talk it over with Father Debakis. Take as long as you need."

Zoe was so thrilled to have been offered

a job it took a minute for her to comprehend it. She fought back her tears. "I'll never be able to thank you enough for this offer, not to mention the generosity of your family's foundation."

He got to his feet. Again she felt his scrutiny. "Be sure it's what you want," he warned in a more serious tone of voice. If she didn't know anything else, she knew deep down this was what she wanted and needed. "In the meantime I have to fly back to Athens tonight. You can phone me when you've made your decision."

Seize the moment, Zoe. "Before you leave, could I ask you a few more questions?"

"Of course."

"What's the weather like right now?"

"It's been in the low eighties all summer and won't drop to the seventies until later in September. Usually the night temperature is in the sixties."

"It sounds too good to be true. Are there shops near the hospital to buy clothes?"

"The center is on the outskirts of the small seaside village of Loggos. There are a few tourist shops, but I'd suggest you do your shopping in Athens first."

"Then that solves any problems I'll have about luggage. I lost everything in the fire so I'll replenish my wardrobe there."

He paused in the doorway, looking surprised. "Does this mean you've already made up your mind?"

She eyed the priest then glanced back at the other man. "I can't wait!"

"I can see you're a woman who knows her own mind." She thought his eyes might be smiling. "Under the circumstances, let's go out for dinner where we can talk over details. I'll drive you back to your shelter then leave for the airport."

She turned to the priest. "Oh, Father Debakis... I'm so happy I could take flight."

He chuckled. "I believe you could."

Vasso knew he'd never forget this moment. It was a nice feeling to make someone happy. He smiled at the priest. "It's been a pleasure to meet you."

"And mine, Kyrie Giannopoulos. Bless you."

"Shall we go, *thespinis*?"

After they walked out to the limo, he asked her to recommend a good place to eat.

Zoe swung around. "There's a Greek diner called Zito's a few blocks over. They serve lamb kebabs and potatoes so soft you can taste the lemon."

That sounded good to him. He told the driver who headed there, then concentrated on the charming female seated across from him. "We need to talk about your travel arrangements. There are dozens of flights to Athens every day. Once we know the date, I'll book a flight for you."

"Thank you, but I'll take care of that. This is so exciting, I can't believe it's happening."

Her excitement was contagious. He hadn't felt this alive in a long time. Once inside the diner they were shown to a table for two. The minute they were seated and Zoe ordered for them, she flicked him a searching glance.

"While I've got you here alone, I need your advice. If I were to take Kyrie Megalos a small gift from New York, what would he like?"

His lips twitched. "He collects naval memorabilia from all over the world."

That gave her a great idea. "Thanks for the tip."

"You're welcome. Before any more time

passes, I need to know about your financial situation."

"I don't have one. I'm broke." A laugh escaped her lips, delighting him. "That doesn't mean I have no money, but it wouldn't be enough to keep me alive for more than a few months. That's why I can't wait to start work.

"When I look back, I'm pretty sure I know the reason why Ms. Kallistos didn't want me to work there. I took up a bed in the center for eight months after my first cancer-free checkup. That's because I was allowed to live in the hospital's long-term facility for the last eight months and get therapy to help me with grief issues."

Vasso surmised that was only one of the reasons Ms. Kallistos had problems with Zoe. No woman could compete with this female's effervescent personality. Her reverence for life sucked you in.

"After the chemo and bone marrow transplant, I was given all the time there I needed to recover, for which I'm grateful. I don't even have to wear a wig now. No one would ever guess that I'd once lost all of it."

Without her blond hair that had a slightly windblown look, she would still possess stunning classic features. "You seem the picture of health. If a long stay at the center was what made the difference in your recovery, then I applaud the therapist's decision."

She nodded. "I finally got it out of my doctor that the therapist was worried about my recovery. Losing my parents was so horrendous I had gone into a deep depression, and he could see I needed counseling. That part was certainly true. I was an only child and way too connected to them at the hip. They were wonderful and worked so hard, I tried to do everything I could to help them. In one night my whole world evaporated."

"That's the way my brother and I felt when our father died of lymphoma. The world we knew had gone away. Luckily we had each other."

"My therapist explained that if I'd had a sibling, it might have made a big difference. He made me realize why I had such a hard time letting them go. Grief hits everyone differently. In my case I was a twenty-four-year-old woman crying like a child for her parents. You don't know how much fun they were. We were best friends."

"Akis and I had the same relationship with

our father." Everything she told Vasso rang so true with him about his own life he had trouble finding words. "I'm glad the priest prevailed on me to interview you. He's very persuasive."

Another quick smile appeared. "He is that. The other day when the doctor saw me for my six-weeks checkup and told me I was still cancer-free, something changed inside of me. I didn't want to stay there any longer and realized I'd come out of the worst of my depression. Father Debakis knew about my wanting to work for your foundation. So for you to give me a chance is like another miracle." Her voice trembled. "Thank you for this opportunity. I promise I won't let you down."

"I'm sure you won't."

The waiter brought their food, but Vasso hardly noticed what he was eating because emotions got in the way of anything else. Their conversation had reminded him of the father he and Akis missed. Their dad had treated them like buddies. He had laughed and joked with them.

Vasso always marveled over how smart he was. Their father knew everyone and had taught them to treat other people with respect. That was how you got ahead. He and Akis remembered everything their father had told them.

She finished her meal before looking up at him. "Your money saved my life and it's saving the lives of everyone at the hospital. Not just the patients, but the staff too. My oncologist is thrilled to be working there. You and your family have done more for others than you will ever know."

"I hear you, Zoe. Now no more talk about gratitude. Because you'll be living on Paxos, I know of several places you can rent. By the time you reach the island, I'll have lined up some apartments for you to look at."

"That's very thoughtful of you, but I can do that myself."

"I'm sure you could, but you'll need a place close to the center and they're not easy to come by."

"Then I take your word for it. Thank you."

"If you've finished, I'll run you by the shelter."

She got up from the table. "I'll phone you as soon as I've made my flight plans."

"I'll be expecting your call and we'll go from there."

As he walked her out to the limo, he felt as if he too had undergone a life-changing experience. Of course he realized the foundation was helping many people. But for the first time since he and his brother had established the two centers, he had a personal interest in one of the former patients who had recovered.

She'd been so open about her family it triggered memories for him about his father and the life the three of them had enjoyed together before he'd died. Despite their poverty they'd had fun, too. He'd forgotten that aspect until Zoe started talking about her life. Because of her comments about family, he was seeing his own past through fresh eyes. Her story tugged at his heart and Vasso found he was no longer the same emotionally closed-up man who'd flown to New York on business.

August 17, Athens, Greece

Prickles of delight broke out on the back of Zoe's neck as the plane made its descent through a cloudless sky toward the runway. From her coach-class window seat she looked out at the sea, the islands. Closer still she made out the clay-roofed houses lining Athens's winding roads. This was Vasso Giannopoulos's world.

A sense of wonderment accompanied these sensations because she still couldn't believe she was coming to a place where she'd never been before and would be working. No doubt her ancestors experienced the same feelings when they arrived in the US, ready to embark on a new life.

How easy her life was by comparison! Instead of reaching the US by ship, she was on an airliner. Instead of having to undergo a holding time for immigrants, she'd been given safe passage right through to the Athens airport where she'd be taken care of. A job was waiting for her. So was the man who'd made all this possible. He was so wonderful she couldn't believe how lucky she was to have met him.

Kyrie Giannopoulos and his family were responsible for everything that had happened to her since she'd been admitted to the Giannopoulos Center in Astoria a year ago. Somehow he'd made it possible for her to work for his foundation. He'd said he'd be waiting for her when her plane landed.

The thought of seeing him again gave her butterflies. Surely meeting him a second time wouldn't cause her legs to almost buckle as they'd done the first time. The mere sight of such a magnificent-looking man had haunted her thoughts whether she was awake or asleep.

After the plane touched down and taxied to the hangar, the seat belt came off and Zoe reached for her secondhand overnight bag. She followed the other passengers out of the plane to the terminal lounge where they went through customs. Her bag was searched. After she'd presented her passport and answered a few questions, a female airline attendant came up to her.

"You're Zoe Zachos?"

"Yes?"

"Come with me, please."

She got on a cart and was driven some distance to an elevator that descended to the ground floor. After another little ride the airline employee stopped the cart in front of a door. She got out and opened it. "Your ride is waiting out there."

The second Zoe walked through the door onto the tarmac where the hot sun beat down she saw a limousine in the distance. Once again her legs seemed to go weak when she spotted her benefactor lounging against the passenger side wearing sunglasses. This morning he'd dressed in a light blue sport shirt and tan chinos. He looked so wonderful she moaned before she realized he could have heard her.

"Thespinis Zachos, welcome to Greece."

No man should be this handsome. Zoe felt out of breath. "Thank you for meeting me."

"Of course. I hope you had a good flight." He took her bag and opened the rear door for her to get in.

"It was fine."

He went around the other side and got in with her bag so they sat across from each other. The interior smelled of the soap he must have used in the shower. Her reaction to him was over the top. Maybe there was something wrong with her.

"My driver will take us to the complex where my brother and I work. We'll stay in the penthouse. It's where we entertain guests and business people who must stay overnight. Tomorrow we'll fly to Paxos."

The limousine moved into the center of Athens. Another time and she might enjoy the scenery more, but right now she couldn't concentrate. After what he'd just told her, Zoe felt like a tongue-tied high school girl with a giant-sized crush on a man so far out of her league it was outrageous.

Glomming onto the safer subject of business she said, "Does Kyrie Megalos know you've hired me?"

"Not yet. I want him to meet you first."

She eyed him directly, but couldn't see his eyes behind the glasses. "Something tells me you're pulling the same thing on him that Father Debakis pulled on you." Vasso laughed hard. "He may not want me to be his assistant."

"In that case he'll give you another position. Don't worry. He won't suggest that you join a nunnery."

Laughter escaped her lips. His sense of humor was very appealing. "I shouldn't have said anything about Ms. Kallistos's remark. It wasn't kind of me."

"She should have known better than to say anything, so put it out of your mind."

"I have. Do you mind if I ask you some questions? Would you please tell me what kind of business you're in? I don't have a lot of information about you apart from your philanthropic work."

They'd driven into the heart of the downtown traffic. "If you'll look out your right window, you'll see a store coming up that says Alpha/Omega 24."

Zoe searched each shop. "Oh—there it is! *Everything from A to Z*. It's like one of the 7-Elevens in the States!"

"It's store number four, the first store we opened on the mainland."

"So you're a convenience store owner! Where are stores one through three?"

"On Paxos. My brother and I started our own chain years ago. They've spread throughout Greece."

"Now you're forcing me to guess." She eyed him with an impish expression. "Do you have as many as a hundred perchance?"

"We reached the hundred mark in Thessalonika."

Zoe gulped. "You weren't kidding, were

you? Does your chain spread as far as Florina?"

"Farther, but it might interest you to know we have a store in Kozani. It's not far from the home of your ancestors."

She'd just been teasing, but he'd come back with an answer that filled her with awe. "So how many stores do you have altogether? Wait—don't answer that question." Heat filled her cheeks. "I'm being rude to pry. Forgive me."

"I don't mind. 2001, including the one we recently opened in Crete."

Zoe had tried to imagine the kind of money it took to run both centers. Now that she knew what kind of wealth was behind the foundation, she was blown away by the generosity of these men. "You really are perfect," she whispered.

"You have a lot to learn," he quipped, making her smile.

By now the limousine had turned down an alley and stopped at the side of a big complex. He got out with her bag and came around to help her. He had a remote on his key chain that opened the door to an elevator. They rode it to the top. When the door opened, she entered a glassed-in penthouse where she welcomed the air conditioning.

"If you'll come with me, I'll show you to the guest bedroom." She followed him through a hallway to a room with a fabulous view of Athens.

"What an incredible vista! Am I the luckiest woman in the world to sleep here tonight or what? You're far too good to me."

"We do this for business people who come to be interviewed for store manager positions."

"But I'm not exactly the kind of business person that generates a profit for you. I promise I'll do my best to help the patients at the hospital."

"I have no doubt of it." He put her overnight bag on the floor. "The en-suite bathroom is through that door. This area of the penthouse is all yours until we leave for Paxos. Now I'm sure you want to freshen up and relax, but first let me show you the kitchen."

She walked down the hallway to the other part of the penthouse with him. "There's food and drink waiting for you if you're hungry. Please help yourself to anything you want while I go down to the office and check in. If you need me, just phone me, but I won't be long. After lunch we can go shopping if you're up to it."

"Thank you, Kyrie Giannopoulos." He was beyond kind and so many other things she'd lost count.

"Call me Vasso."

She smiled. "I'm Zoe."

He'd removed his sunglasses. "Zoe Zachos. Has anyone ever called you ZZ?"

Another laugh broke from her. He had a bit of an imp in him. "No. You're the first."

She felt the warmth from his black eyes long after he'd left the penthouse. Before doing anything else she walked over to the windows in the living room. The site of the Acropolis seemed as surreal as the whole experience of meeting Vasso Giannopoulos for the first time.

He had to be a very busy man, yet he'd taken time out to interview her himself. His insight about the emotions she would experience by moving to Greece revealed he was a man of empathy and compassion. Because of his goodness, her life was already being transformed.

CHAPTER THREE

"KYRIE GIANNOPOULOS?" VASSO'S secretary spoke to him as he was passing through to his office. "Your brother said he'd be in after lunch. You've had two calls this morning from Maris Paulos who said it was urgent you get back to her."

In order to maintain his privacy, he gave out his cell phone number only to a few people. It forced Maris to reach him through his secretary. Until she'd mentioned Maris's name, Vasso hadn't thought about her.

"I'll call her now. Just so you know I'll be out of the office tomorrow. Akis will handle anything that comes up. If there's an emergency, he'll call me."

"Yes, sir."

Vasso went into his private office and rang Maris. After apologizing for not phoning her before his quick trip to New York, he asked if they could meet later that night. He'd stop by her condo. She sounded happy. That worried him because he didn't plan on seeing her after tonight. But Maris deserved the truth. She wanted more out of their relationship, but he didn't have it inside to give.

With that taken care of, he sequestered himself in his office for a couple of hours to do paperwork. Then he phoned Zoe.

"I'm glad you called. I've eaten lunch and was just leaving to go shopping."

"Then I'll take you."

"Oh no. You've done enough for me."

She was so different from other women he'd known whose interest in money seemed to be at the forefront. Both he and Akis felt the women they met were always assessing the worth of the Giannopoulos brothers, a real turnoff. But the Zoe he'd met so far seemed the exact opposite of a woman with that kind of hidden agenda.

"But you don't know where to go to shop."

"I'll be fine. I've lived in a big city all my life."

Vasso chuckled at her show of independence. "I realize that. But it would please me to accompany you this once. I'm coming upstairs now."

He was aware how grateful she was for everything. Pleased that she wasn't too tired, he arranged for his driver to meet them in the alley and drive them to the Attica department store near Syntagma Square.

She must have showered because she smelled sweet like a fragrant rose, dressed in a different skirt and blouse, when he helped her out of the limo. "You'll find everything you want here at a good price," he explained. "Shall we start in the luggage department? You'll need a large suitcase."

Her sculpted mouth curved into a smile. "You're reading my mind."

He liked the three-piece set of luggage she picked with a gold fleur-de-lis design on a dark red background. Vasso asked the clerk to find an employee to take their purchases out to the limousine waiting in front of the store.

Women's clothing was on the next floor. Zoe stopped him before they approached the counter. "Tell me something honestly. I saw Ms. Kallistos coming and going for a whole year. She only wore dresses or skirts and blouses. Would you suggest the same thing for me?"

"For work, yes. But you'll want other kinds of clothes, too. The island has a lot to offer when you're off of work. Among other things like jeans and shorts, you're going to need some good walking shoes and a bathing suit. Maybe a sweater or jacket when the nights cool down. Paxos is a different world from New York."

"I realize that. After living in the asphalt jungle, I'm relishing the quiet of a sun-filled island with no skyscrapers."

"You're going to undergo a big change. Tell me something. Do you have a laptop?"

"I had one for college, but it got destroyed in the fire."

"I was afraid that might be the case."

"Stop, Vasso. I know what you're going to say. I have enough money to buy another one."

"I believe you, but the foundation supplies all the equipment, so I have an idea. While you shop for clothes, I'll go to the electronics department and get you a computer. You'll need it when you're not at the center.

It shouldn't take me long then I'll come back here for you."

"That sounds good. When we're through shopping, I'd like to take you to an early dinner. It will be on me. I'm afraid I won't have much money left to spend, so I'll let you pick a place my pathetic bank account can afford."

Those shimmering green eyes had him mesmerized. "I know just a spot in the Plaka. You'll love it."

"The old part of Athens," she mused. "To think I have Greek blood running through my veins, yet I've never been here. I promise to hurry because I can't wait to explore." Zoe's eagerness to live life made him see it through new eyes. "My father didn't like to go shopping with my mother because she took so long. I'll try not to be like her."

Amused by the comment he said, "Take all the time you need." He and Akis had grown up in a one-parent household, so he didn't know what it would be like to hear two parents going at it back and forth.

He left her talking to a saleswoman and headed for another part of the store. Besides a laptop, Vasso wanted her to have a new iPhone. He was still amazed by the extent of her loss, and even more astounded that she wasn't bitter or angry. She didn't know how to feel sorry for herself. That trait alone increased his admiration for her.

Fire had snatched away everything from her, including her parents. She was forced to build a life all over again. The woman was a survivor in more ways than one. He couldn't imagine another woman of his acquaintance who would be eager to throw herself headlong into an undetermined future.

She was beautiful inside and out. By some miracle the lymphoma hadn't taken her life. Her gratitude was over the top, yet it was that very quality that drew him to her. You couldn't compare her to anyone else. She'd maintained a great sense of humor even after the ordeal she'd been through, which put her in a class by herself.

As Vasso had discussed with Akis, he was happy they'd honored their father by creating the foundation. But at the time, neither of them had any idea that their money would be responsible for Zoe getting the medical care she'd needed to whip the terrible disease. Today he was thankful they'd had both centers built so he could give her the job she wanted.

She's becoming important to you.

An hour later he found her and they walked out of the store with their arms loaded. They were greeted by a rash of photographers and journalists taking pictures and calling out questions. Someone had tipped the paparazzi off that he'd come to the store. Vasso was furious this had happened, but Zoe seemed to handle it well by ignoring them. He helped her into the smoked-glass limo.

"You must be a celebrity," she said in a quiet voice.

"Anyone's a celebrity if they have money."

"There's a lot more to their interest in you than that!"

"It's because Akis and I came from a life of poverty. The media has been following us around for several years."

"How ghastly." He heard a sigh come out of her. "But I think it's because you've done something extraordinary with your lives. To impart your fortune for the good of humanity puts you in a class all by yourselves. Surely you must realize how much people admire you for that. It's a great compliment to you, even if you don't like the publicity."

"Trust me, I don't," he muttered. "Let's forget them. I'm just sorry I couldn't protect you from them."

"I can understand that you don't relish being mobbed."

She understood a lot of things that made him feel closer to her. He was beginning to desire her company more and more. "It's one of the reasons why I don't spend all my time in Athens."

Her gaze darted to him. "I don't blame you. Under the circumstances, can we go back to the penthouse to eat dinner? Now that they've seen you, they'll probably follow us to the Plaka. If I can't pay for our meal, I can at least cook for you."

"I didn't bring you here to cook."

"You don't know how much I miss it. I was at the center for a whole year. No place of my own to have fun in the kitchen. Yours is a cook's dream, believe me! But please don't misunderstand me," she cried softly. "I just meant that now I'm well, I look forward to doing the things that once brought me pleasure. That is if you'll let me."

How could he say no to that? "Of course."

"If I say so myself, my parents' *taverna* brought in a lot of customers because of my mother's recipes that go way back."

Vasso couldn't hear enough about her life. "What was her specialty?"

"She had several, but my favorite main dish is *burek*."

His brows lifted. "You can make Macedonian *burek*?"

"So you like it?" Her eyes smiled.

"I had it once in Kozani and loved it."

"I'd like to make it for you if you'll let me loose in your kitchen. We'll see how it compares. But you need to start with an appetizer and some Mastika liqueur over ice. You probably don't have any of that on hand."

"Our number-four store should carry it. We'll stop there on the way back."

She reached in her purse and wrote something on a piece of paper before handing it to him. "Do you have all these items?"

He checked the list: dough ingredients, minced lamb, white cheese, spinach, *kasseri* yellow cheese, olives and tomatoes. They'd need to pick up at least half the items on her list. Vasso alerted his driver, then focused on her. "I'm already salivating."

"So am I." She chuckled. "There's nothing I'd love more than to fix you one of my family's specialties."

"Are you homesick for New York already?" He'd been worrying about that. To live on Paxos was going to be a huge adjustment for her.

"I'll never stop missing my parents, but there's nothing in New York for me now so I won't be missing it. Yet being able to cook up a meal in your kitchen will be a little like old times with my folks."

Her tremulous answer tugged on his emotions. He had a longing to comfort her. "I can relate. So many times I've wanted to discuss business with our father."

"Every time I went into the hospital chapel, I would read the words on the plaque and wonder about him. When did he die?"

"Sixteen years ago."

She shook her head. "You were so young to lose him. That must have been terribly hard on your mother."

Vasso cleared his throat. "She died soon after I was born."

A slight gasp escaped her. "I had no idea. That means your father raised you and your brother alone. Did you have grandparents?"

"They died too, but that's another story."

"Will you tell me about it?"

"Maybe. Over dinner." Just then the limo pulled in front of the store. "I'll be right back." He got out and hurried inside the crowded interior.

"Boss?"

"*Yassou,* Galen. I'm here to pick up a bottle of Mastika liqueur."

"I think we've got one left. It's been on the top shelf in back for a while."

"The older, the better."

"I'll get it."

"Let me." Vasso found it and the other items needed. After putting some bills on the counter he said, "Talk to you later."

When he got back in the limo with the groceries, he handed the bottle to Zoe. "Is this what you wanted?"

She looked delighted. "I can't believe you stock it here. No wonder your stores have been such a huge success. This is my lucky day. Now I'm going to have to produce a meal that will win the Giannopoulos seal of approval."

He laughed, realizing that she had a knack for bringing that out in him. When she'd walked into Alexandra's office last week, he hadn't been prepared for the effect this utterly feminine woman would have on him. But the first impression she'd made on him, with her wavy blond hair, had brought a spring-like newness into his life.

When they arrived at the penthouse, they loaded everything into the elevator and rode to the top. Before long they'd taken everything to her bedroom. Then they gravitated to the kitchen where he helped her gather all the ingredients to make their dinner.

It was fun working side by side. "This is a brand-new experience for me."

"How come?"

"I've never brought a woman to the penthouse, let alone allowed her to take over the kitchen."

"You're kidding! Not one girlfriend?"

"I have a confession to make. After Akis and I started making real money, we worried whether the women we met only wanted us for what we could do for them. We refused to bring them here. It was safer to take them to dinner. That probably sounds very cynical to you."

"No. Not after what you've told me about your life. There's a lot of avarice in the world. I imagine anyone who has the kind of money you make would have trouble trusting someone who wanted to get close to him."

"Akis had the same trust issues, but he's married now. When he first met Raina, he fell hard. But his fear of not being loved for himself caused him all sorts of pain."

"How did they meet?"

"She flew over to attend the wedding reception of her Greek friend Chloe who'd lived with her in California. Akis had been the best man. After running away from the maid of honor who was after him, he picked on Raina to dance with him until he could get out of the room safely. That accidental meeting changed his life."

Zoe chuckled. "When did he know she was the real thing?"

"He always knew it in his heart, but he needed a nudge. I did some research on her and learned she was Raina Maywood."

"What? Isn't she the famous American heiress to the Maywood fortune?"

He nodded. "When Akis found out, everything changed. He knew that she wasn't after his money, but he had another problem."

"Why?"

"He didn't feel good enough for her. Our lack of formal education made him worry that she'd soon grow bored of him. On the night she was leaving to go back to California, I called her and begged her to go to him. She was broken up, not understanding why he couldn't accept that she loved him. Luckily she took my advice and convinced him he was her whole world. They got married fast and I've never seen him so happy."

"Was that a little hard on you?"

He looked in those compassionate green eyes. "You have a lot of insight, Zoe. Until they said their vows, I never realized how connected we'd been throughout our lives. When you told me how close you were to your parents, you were describing me and Akis.

"I felt lost at first, but slowly that feeling started to dissipate. Raina has been a joy and makes my little brother so happy I can't imagine life without her now. With a baby on the way, Akis isn't the same man."

"A baby? That's wonderful!"

"When Akis and I were young and struggling, we couldn't have imagined this day."

She flashed him a smile. "And now there's a lot more to come. Your lives are a miracle, too."

The things she said...

They kept working in harmony. Zoe definitely knew her way around a kitchen. By seven o'clock, they sat down at the dining room table to eat the best home-cooked food he'd ever tasted.

They started with the Mastika poured over ice and served with a grilled *krusevo* cheese pie for an appetizer. The *burek* was out of this world. Layers of dough with white cheese, minced lamb and spinach garnished with tomatoes and onions marinated in a special herb sauce. It was so good he ate more than he normally did at a meal.

"You could open your own *taverna*, Zoe."

"What a lovely compliment. Before I decided to go to college, I actually thought about it, but my parents insisted I try college first. You know the rest. Then the day came when the world as I knew it went away."

Vasso didn't want her to think sad thoughts. "We can be thankful you didn't go away with it or I wouldn't have been treated to such a feast."

"You're just being nice."

"Not true. Now it's my turn to pay you back by doing the dishes while you get your bags packed. Tomorrow we'll have breakfast here and fly to Paxos."

That was the plan, but he discovered he was loving her company so much he wanted to keep her here in Athens for a while and show her around. It shocked him that he could feel this attracted when they'd known each other for such a short while. How had he existed all this time before she came into his life?

"Before I do that, I want to hear about your grandparents. It's sad to think you didn't have them in your life either." She started clearing the table. It thrilled him she didn't want to leave him quite yet.

"Both sets of grandparents came from Paxos."

"Ah. I'm beginning to understand why the island has been so important to you."

"The grandparents on my father's side and their children—with the exception of our father—were victims of the malaria epidemic on Paxos. In the early sixties it was eradicated, but they didn't escape it."

"Amazing that your father didn't get the disease."

"No. Pockets of people were spared. No one knows why. Maybe he was naturally immune. A poor fisherman who lived on Paxos took care of my father. Together they caught and sold fish at the market in Loggos.

"After the fisherman died, our father continued to fish in the man's rowboat. It was in town he met our mother. She and her brother Kristos survived the epidemic that had killed her family. He emigrated to New York to find a new life, but was killed crossing a busy street."

"How awful. That explains his name on the plaque!"

"Yes. Apparently my mother grieved when he left Greece. In time she and my father fell in love and got married. She worked in the olive groves. Together they scraped to make ends meet any way they could.

"I was born first. Then Akis came along eleven months later. But the delivery was too hard on *Mama* who was in frail health and she died."

He could see Zoe was trying not to break down. "It pains me that neither of you knew your mother. That's so tragic. I at least didn't lose my parents until a year ago, so I have all the memories of growing up with them."

His eyes met hers. "In ways I think your pain has been much worse. We never knew her. She didn't know about her brother getting killed, which was a good thing. We were so young when she died we had no memories except the ones our father told us about. But you lived, laughed and cried with your parents for your whole life, doing everything together. That's a loss I can't comprehend."

"Thanks to the therapy provided by your generosity, I'm doing fine these days. Truly your father had to be a saint to manage on his own. No wonder you wanted to do something extraordinary to honor his name."

"To be sure, he was our hero. I was six when we helped him in the store where he sold the fish. Neither Akis nor I went to school regularly because we needed the money too badly. Poverty was all my father knew. I know it hurt his pride that we boys were known as the poor Giannopoulos kids.

"Most people looked down on us. But no one could know the depth of our pain when he was diagnosed with lymphoma and died. At that point we only had each other in order to survive. *Papa* asked me to look out for Akis."

Zoe gasped. "How old were you?"

"Thirteen and fourteen."

"Overnight you two had to become men."

"All we knew was that we only had ourselves in order to survive. The man who owned the store died and his wife needed help. We asked if we could stay on and work for her. By then the woman was used to us and she really needed the help. So she let us work in her store.

"Akis and I traded off jobs. He'd wait on the customers while I went fishing and picked olives. Then we'd turn the schedule around. We worked long hours."

"When did you fit in some time to play, let alone attend school?"

"Not very often."

"I'd love to meet Akis."

"That can be arranged. But enough about me. Now I want to change the subject. Have you ever ridden in a helicopter?"

She shook her head, still haunted by what he'd told her. "No. I've always wondered what it would be like."

"Does the thought of it make you nervous?"

"Kind of." A hint of smile broke the corner of her mouth. "Ask me tomorrow when I actually have to climb inside it."

"Once you get used to it, you won't want to travel any other way."

"I'll have to take your word for it." After a hesitation… "Vasso?"

He'd started loading the dishwasher. "What is it?"

"You've been so kind to me my debt to you keeps growing. I told Father Debakis what I'm going to tell you. If it takes me the rest of my life, and it probably will, I intend to pay back every cent your foundation spent on my behalf.

"Every inmate at the center would like to tell you of their gratitude in person. You've saved the lives of many people who had no hope. It's staggering the good you've already done." Her lower lip started to tremble. "You're wonderful."

Her words moved him. "If I started to tell you all the things I think about you, there wouldn't be enough hours."

Color rushed into her cheeks. "You're full of it, but it's nice to hear."

"How could the man you had been seeing before the fire have walked away?" he whispered. That question had been gnawing at him since she'd first told him she'd had a boyfriend.

"I don't know." She half laughed as she said it. "He broke my heart when he made the decision to move to Boston. I went through a lot of pain, but with hindsight I can see he didn't love me in that heart-whole way or he couldn't have left.

"After several months I decided I was lucky. If there'd been no fire, would he have eventually asked me to marry him? I don't have an answer. But the fact remains that he wanted to go to Boston more than he wanted to be with me. I certainly don't blame him. To be with a terminally ill patient would mean he had to forget his dreams. That's asking too much of a man unless he's met the love of his life."

"Was he the love of *your* life?" Vasso needed to hear her answer.

"Let me put it this way. I had boyfriends. Some meant more to me than others. But I met Chad while we were both on that study abroad program in England. That was his graduation-from-college present. It threw us together for two weeks. You can learn a lot about someone on a trip like that. We had fun and didn't want it to end after we returned to New York.

"The more I saw of him, the more I thought maybe he could be *the* one. But the circumstances that brought me to this hospital put an end to the relationship we'd enjoyed. Now you know the story of my life."

"But not the pain you suffered when he didn't stay with you."

She took a deep breath. "It was awful. I won't lie about that. If ever I needed someone who loved me that was the time. But his love wasn't the forever kind. That was a hard lesson to learn. It taught me not to put my faith in a man." She looked up at him. "That's as honest as I know how to be."

The man had been a fool. Vasso's black eyes burned into hers. "Just look what he missed. Thank you for telling me."

"I've probably said too much." After taking a few steps away from him, she turned around. "Thanks for listening. I've talked your ear off."

"It was my pleasure. Just so you know, I have to go out again for a little while. I'll try not to disturb you when I come back in."

"Please don't worry about me. Good night." In the next instant she'd disappeared into the other part of the penthouse.

While Vasso stood there overwhelmed by tender new feelings she brought out in him, his cell rang. He pulled it from his pocket. When he saw it was his brother, he clicked on. "Akis?"

"I thought I'd check in. How's everything going with Thespinis Zachos?"

He held his breath. "Fine."

Low laughter bubbled out of Akis. "Come on. It's *me* you're talking to."

"I'm aware of that. I took her shopping,

then we had dinner and now she's gone to bed. Tomorrow morning we'll fly to Paxos."

"I can read between the lines, bro. Let's try this again. How are things really going?"

"The press intruded as we left the department store, so we came back to the penthouse and she cooked dinner. It was probably the best Macedonian food I've ever eaten."

"I guess that makes sense considering her parents ran a *taverna*."

"She only has one more semester before she receives her college degree in English, but Alexandra didn't know about that. It's just as well Zoe will be working on this side of the Atlantic. Tonight she told me she wants to meet you and thank you for saving her life. If you want my opinion, she'll charm Yiannis until she has him eating out of her hand."

"It wouldn't surprise me considering she's already accomplished that feat with you. A woman cooking in our kitchen? That has to be a first. I guess it's too late to tell you to go slow, the same advice you once gave me. *Kalinihta*."

"*Kalinihta*."

Zoe was still on his mind when he arrived at Maris's condo twenty minutes later.

"Vasso—you're finally here!" she said after opening the door. "I've missed you."

But when she would have reached for him, he backed away.

A hurt look entered her eyes. "What's wrong?"

Vasso hated to do this, but for both their sakes he needed to break things off with her. Zoe filled his thoughts to the exclusion of all else, but that made him anxious when he remembered how he'd once felt about Sofia.

As for Maris, he didn't like hurting her when she'd done nothing wrong, but as he'd told his brother, she wasn't the one. Still, he couldn't help feeling a little guilty about doing this to her.

"Let's sit down."

"I don't want to." Her chin lifted. "Why do I get the feeling you're here to tell me it's over with us?"

Being a journalist, she had good instincts and was always out for the truth. "To be honest, while I was in New York I had a chance to think. I don't believe there's a future for us and I thought it would be better to tell you now. I like you very much, Maris. We've had some good times, but—"

"But you're ready to move on," she interrupted him.

"Surely you know I don't mean to hurt you."

"One of my friends told me this was how it would end with you, but I didn't want to believe her. So who's the new woman in the life of the famous Vasso Giannopoulos?"

He stared her down. "Would you have preferred that I told you this over the phone?"

She had the grace to shake her head. "No. It hurts no matter what."

Vasso admired her honesty. "I've enjoyed the times we've spent together and I wish you the very best in the future."

Maris walked over to the door and opened it. "I'm afraid I can't wish you the same, but one day I'll get over it. I thought we had a real connection. Being with you has meant everything to me. Too bad it was one-sided. *Adio,* Vasso."

He left for the penthouse. After reflecting on what had just happened at Maris's condo, he realized this had been the story of his life since Sofia Peri had rejected his marriage proposal. That was ten years ago after he'd finished his military service. It had taken a long time to get over the pain of her marrying someone else. From then on he'd buried himself in business with Akis.

Over the last few years he'd been with different women when time permitted, but he'd ended every relationship prematurely and had pretty well given up on finding his soul mate.

Then Zoe Zachos had walked in Alexandra's office, causing his heart to beat so hard he hadn't been the same since. In the last twenty-four hours her effect on him had been staggering.

After getting used to being in a helicopter, Zoe was entranced by everything she saw. They passed over so many historic places in the Ionian Sea she'd only read about in books or seen in the movies she was awestruck.

From the copilot's seat, Vasso looked back at her through his sunglasses. Today he'd dressed in a white crewneck and white cargo pants. It wasn't fair one man out of millions could be so attractive. Using the mic he said, "We're coming up on Paxos."

She looked down from the window. "But it's so tiny!"

"It's only seven miles by three. Too small for an airport which is just the way all of us who live on the island like it."

Zoe leaned forward. "What do you mean *we?*"

A dazzling white smile greeted her gaze. "As I told you last night, my brother and I were born here. We had the center built here. *My* home is here."

Her heart pounded so hard she was afraid he could hear it. "*This* is where you live when you're not in Athens or traveling for business?"

"That's right."

In shock that she'd be working so close to this fantastic man's home, she turned to the window once more.

"We're flying to the center now. I've phoned Yiannis to expect me. Once inside his office you two can meet and talk about the position."

As the helicopter dipped, she made out several fishing villages with colorful harbors. Lower and lower now, she took in the lush deep greenery of olive trees sprinkled with pastel-colored clusters of small villas. Quaint waterside cottages came into view.

One stretch of fine white sand scalloped the green coves and gave way to another seaside village. On the outskirts now she realized they were headed for a sprawling white complex peeking out of the olive groves.

She held her breath as they were about to land. This time it set down on the hospital roof, but she wasn't as nervous as when the helicopter had lifted off the penthouse roof.

"Are you all right, Zoe?"

"Yes. I was just thinking how my parents and I would have loved transportation like this all the years we lived in New York City. I'm spoiled already."

But the minute the words were out of her mouth, it made her realize she did too much talking. He brought that out in her. Now that they'd landed, she didn't want to prolong the conversation and unbuckled her seat belt.

She thanked the pilot and climbed out of the helicopter wearing one of her new outfits. The navy cotton dress with the white print had a crew neck and sleeves to the elbow. It was summery light, yet had a certain classy look she felt would be appropriate for the job.

When Vasso walked her to the stairs that led to an elevator, she felt his gaze travel over her. Hopefully he approved of her choice of dress. But the second Zoe entertained the thought she was irritated with herself that he was on her mind way too much. The fact that his home was so close to the center meant she'd probably see him more often than she would have imagined. It shouldn't thrill her so much.

"This is a private elevator," he explained as they entered. "The hospital takes up three floors. On the second floor there's a walkway to the three-floor convalescent center. Yiannis's office is on the main floor off the foyer at the main entrance."

They exited the elevator and walked along the corridor of one wing, passing a set of doors with stained-glass inserts signifying the chapel. Zoe looked around. "I love the Hellenic architecture." Their eyes met for a moment. "It flows like the sculpture of a Greek temple."

Her comment seemed to please him. "When we had it built, we tried to preserve the flavor of the island. The kitchen and cafeteria are in the other wing. The eating area extends outside the doors to the patio overlooking the water."

"A hospital built in the middle of paradise," she mused aloud. "If I'd been privileged to recover here, I know I would have lived on the patio. To be near the sea would be heavenly."

When they came to the foyer filled with exotic plants and tubs of flowers, he smiled warmly at a woman probably fifty years old who appeared to run the reception area. "Hebe." He kissed her cheek.

The other woman beamed. "Yiannis said you were coming. It's always good to see you."

"The feeling is mutual. Kyria Lasko, I'd like you to meet Thespinis Zoe Zachos from New York City. She's here for an interview with Yiannis."

"Ah? I hope it means what I think it means." Her friendly brown eyes were so welcoming Zoe was able to relax a little.

"How do you do, Kyria Lasko?" She shook hands with her.

"Call me Hebe."

After being around a cold Alexandra for a whole year, Hebe Lasko was like a breath of fresh air. "Thank you."

"Hebe is the head of our business office located down the other hall," he explained, "but she's been doing double duty as Yiannis's assistant."

Zoe turned to him. "You mean this front desk is where I would work?" she asked quietly.

He nodded. "Yiannis's office is through that door behind the desk. Let's go."

She followed him around the counter where he knocked on the door and was told to enter. Vasso ushered her inside and her first thought was that she'd entered a room in a naval museum.

There were models of ships on the shelving and several framed photographs of the former military leader in dress uniform. Other small photographs showed him with his striking wife. What an attractive man he was with gray hair and dark brown eyes!

As the two men embraced, she noticed he was shorter than Vasso and was dressed in a short-sleeved white shirt and dark trousers. They exchanged comments and his hearty laugh filled the office. Then his eyes swerved to Zoe.

"So, Vasso… I see you've brought along a visitor. A very lovely one at that. Is this some kind of announcement you're making?"

CHAPTER FOUR

THE INFERENCE COULDN'T have been more obvious. Zoe tried to repress a groan.

"In a way, yes! I've found you the assistant you've been needing. Yiannis? Meet Thespinis Zoe Zachos. She was born and raised in New York City, and she's a bilingual Greek American. I was so impressed with her I plucked her away and brought her here. I'm going to leave the two of you to get acquainted and take a look around the facility, but I'll be back."

He disappeared so fast Zoe felt like the foundation had just been knocked out from under her.

The older man smiled at her. "Sit down, Zoe. How come you're still *thespinis*?"

He immediately reminded her of her father

who was always outspoken. "I haven't met the right man yet."

He frowned before taking his seat. "What's wrong with the men in New York?"

"I'm afraid the problem lies with me."

"What are you? Twenty-two?" he asked with a teasing smile.

"I'll be twenty-five next weekend."

His brows lifted. "That old." Laughter broke from her. "All right. Let's start from the beginning. Vasso wouldn't do this to me if he weren't a hundred-percent sure you're the person I'm looking for to help me run this place. Tell me about your background."

Without going into too much unnecessary detail, she told him about her family and education. When she got to the part about the fire, she managed to stay composed. Then she told him about her lymphoma and the year she'd spent at the center.

"My family priest knew how much I wanted to work for the center to pay back all it had done for me. When the doctor gave me another clean bill of health, Father Debakis arranged for Kyrie Giannopoulos to interview me. He said your assistant had to leave and you were looking for a new one."

The older man suddenly sat forward. "You're cancer-free?"

"At the moment, yes. But there's no guaran—"

"Forget that," he broke in on her. "You're exactly what's been needed around here. How long before you have to go back to New York?"

"I—I don't plan to," she stammered. "I told Kyrie Giannopoulos I'd like to work for the foundation for the rest of my life. It will take that long to pay his family back for all they've done for me. If I'm given a job here, this is where I'll plant new roots."

"You're hired, Thespinis Zachos."

Zoe couldn't believe it. "But you hardly know anything about me."

"Of course I do. Vasso wouldn't have brought you here if he had any questions. This center needs input. Who better than you to see what we're doing right or wrong? When I was in the navy, we had informers who quietly gathered information helpful to the brass. With you around, I'm already feeling like I'm back on duty with a crew I can count on."

To hide her joy that he'd accepted her on Vasso's say-so alone, she reached in her tote bag and pulled out a seven-by-seven-inch box wrapped in paper showing various American naval frigates. "This is for you." She handed it to him. "I would have given it to you whether I got the job or not."

Yiannis eyed her in surprise before opening it. "What's this?" He pulled out a creamware mug and read aloud the words printed in dark red ink. *"We have met the enemy and they are ours."*

"That's the image of Edward Preble," she explained. "He was a naval hero at the time of the war in Tripoli. Kyrie Giannopoulos told me you're a naval hero and have collected naval memorabilia. I knew he meant Greek memorabilia, but I thought you could add this mug as a piece to show your appreciation for an American naval hero. A little diversity makes things more interesting, don't you think? If nothing else, you could drink coffee from it."

He burst into laughter at the same moment Vasso joined them. "It looks like you two are getting along famously."

Yiannis lifted the mug. "Did you see this?"

"No."

"Take a look. Our new employee just pre-

sented me a gift to add to my collection."
Vasso shot her a knowing glance before he
took it to examine.

The retired admiral sat back in his chair,
eyeing the two of them with satisfaction.
"The only thing I need to ask now is: how
soon can you come to work? I needed you
yesterday. Poor Hebe has been run ragged
doing the job of two people."

Zoe liked him a lot already. For years she'd
worked with her parents at the *taverna*. It
would be nice to feel useful again with someone dynamic like him. Despite his grief over
the loss of his wife, he had a buoyant spirit.

"Tomorrow morning? Today I need to find
a place to live."

"Tomorrow at eight-thirty it is. You've
made my day."

She got to her feet. "You've made mine
by being willing to give me a chance. I can't
thank you enough and I'll try not to make
you sorry." Zoe shook his hand and headed
for the door. She needed to use the restroom
she'd seen down the hall.

After she emerged, Vasso caught up to her.
"We'll fly back to my house for the car and
drive into Loggos. When we reach the vil-

lage I thought we'd stop for lunch and check out several furnished apartments I told you about. Hopefully one will suit."

Things were moving so fast she could hardly think. "Do all the people working at the center live in Loggos?"

"They come from all over the island, but Loggos is a good place for you to start out. The only bus picks up passengers in front of the main *taverna* and will bring you to the center. It makes three stops a day there in front of the fountain, so you'll always have a ride home. I suggest you give it a month. If it isn't to your liking, you can live wherever you want on the island, but you'll need a car. I'll help you with that when you're ready."

"Thank you, but I don't have a driver's license, Vasso. If I decide to buy a car, then I'll have to take lessons first." He'd already spoiled her so completely she would never be out of his debt. Vasso was so caring and concerned—the differences between him and Chad were like day and night.

The flight back to his house passed in a blur. There was too much to absorb. She couldn't take it all in. Once again she felt the helicopter dip and fly toward a charming, solitary white beach villa with a red tiled roof. They landed on a pad in the middle of a copse of olive trees, causing her breath to escape. There was no doubt in her mind this was Vasso's sanctuary.

She spotted a dark gray Lexus parked nearby.

Once the rotors stopped spinning, Vasso unbuckled the seat belt. While he removed her luggage, she jumped down so he wouldn't have to help her and reached for the train case. Without waiting for him, she headed for his car.

"Zoe? The house is in the other direction. Where do you think you're going?"

"To get in your car. I'm assuming I'll be able to move into an apartment today and don't want to put you out any more than necessary."

"We're not in that big a hurry."

"*I* am. Once I have a place to live and am on the job, I'm going to feel free. I don't expect you to understand. But being the recipient of so much generosity for so long has become a burden, if that makes sense. I hope I haven't offended you."

"Not at all."

Zoe tried to sound matter of fact about it,

but it was hard to hide the sudden alarm that had gripped her. Vasso was already bigger than life to her. She'd been in the penthouse that he and his brother used for business. She'd even cooked a meal there! Because she was a future employee, Vasso had opened every door for her.

But to enter his home would be crossing a line into his private world she refused to consider. She might like it too much. No way did she dare make a move like that. Already she was afraid that her feelings for him might interfere with their professional relationship.

Yiannis Megalos had made an assumption about her and Vasso the second he'd seen them walk in the office. She could imagine how it looked. Obviously Vasso had gone out of his way to do something unprecedented to accommodate her desire to work for the foundation. But this last favor to help her get settled had to be the end of it. Her self-preservation instinct had kicked in to guard her heart.

If she came to depend on Vasso, how did she know he wouldn't be like Chad in the sense that he wasn't invested in the relationship to the extent that she was? Zoe refused to put her trust in a man again where it came to her heart. There was no point anyway since her cancer could be coming back. Better to concentrate on her work and give it her all. In the end she'd be spared a lot of heartache.

She waited for Vasso to bring the rest of her luggage to the car. He used a remote to open the doors and put the luggage in the trunk. Zoe took advantage of the time to get in the front seat.

When he got behind the wheel, he turned to her. Suddenly they were too close. She was so aware of him she could hardly breathe. "Why do you think you would be putting me out?"

Until now she hadn't felt any tension between them, but after what he'd just said, she feared she'd irritated him after all. "Because you've done so much for me, it doesn't make sense that you'll have to come back here later for my luggage."

"I'm in no hurry. Have I led you to believe that?"

She moistened her lips nervously. "No. Of

course not. You're such a gentleman you'd never make anyone uncomfortable. But you and your brother run a huge corporation. Everything was going smoothly until you were asked to interview me. I know Father Debakis laid a big guilt trip on you, so don't try to deny it."

"I wasn't going to."

She took a breath. "Thank you. Since then you've had to deal with me. As if I'm not already indebted to you several hundred thousand dollars."

"Zoe—have you considered the situation from our point of view? Our father died a terrible death while Akis and I stood by helplessly. To know that the foundation has helped someone like you means everything to us. It's a pleasure to see you get back on your feet."

Her head bowed. "You're the two best men I know."

"That's nice to hear. What do you say we drive to the village? After lunch you can take a look at the furnished apartments available. One is over a bakery, the other over a gift shop."

She flicked him a worried glance. "A bakery?"

* * *

The second Zoe's question was out, Vasso realized where he'd gone wrong and gripped the steering wheel so hard it was a miracle he didn't break it. "Forgive me for forgetting where you'd lived." She'd never forget the fire that had traveled to the kitchen of her parents' *taverna*.

"We'll cross that one off the list. You'll like Kyria Panos. She's a widow who's been renting the apartment over the gift shop since her son got married. You'll have your own entrance in the back. The only drawback is that it's a one-bedroom apartment."

"I don't need more than one."

"You're so easy to please it's scary."

"Not all the time."

"Give me an example."

"If I told you some of my hang-ups, you'd send me back to New York on the next flight."

"How about just one?"

"A couple of my girlfriends wanted me to room with them in college, but I'd always had my own space at home and didn't want to give it up. They teased me about it and tried to talk me into it. But the more they tried, the more I didn't like it. I guess I'm really a private person and get prickly when I sense my space is being invaded. That's why I lived with my parents."

"There's nothing wrong with that. But maybe the day will come when you won't want to be alone."

"If you're talking about marriage, I'm not planning on getting married."

"Why?"

"I like my life the way it is." She turned to him. "I really like the way it is right now. I don't want some man bossing me around. One of the older patients at the center used to tell me about the fights she had with her husband. For the most part my parents got along great, so I couldn't relate to this woman's life. He pecked at her all day long."

Vasso's black brows lifted. "Pecked?"

"Yes. You know. Like a hen pecks at her food. That's what he'd do to her about everything. What she bought, what she ate, what she did with her spare time. Peck, peck, peck."

Laughter pealed out of Vasso. "Most of the older women in the center made similar comments about married life. I decided I was well enough off being on my own."

"My brother loves married life."

"Maybe that's true, but what does his wife have to say when he's not listening?"

She heard a chuckle. "I have no idea."

"Maybe it's better you don't know." He laughed louder. She loved hearing it. "I could see in Yiannis's eyes that he wonders why you aren't married, Vasso. Admit you don't want some wife leading you around by the nose."

"Now there's a thought."

She laughed. "I'm only teasing." No woman would ever do that with a man like him. The female who caught his eye would be the luckiest one on the planet. No way did she dare dream about a romantic relationship with Vasso.

If it didn't work out, she wouldn't be able to handle it. Just admitting that to herself proved that her feelings for Vasso already ran deeper than those she'd had for Chad. The two men weren't comparable. No one could ever measure up to Vasso.

"You may be teasing, but I can hear the underlying half truths."

Time to change the subject. "Tell me about my landlady, Kyria Panos. Did she henpeck her husband?"

"As I recall they did a lot of shouting, but for the most part it was good-natured."

"That's nice. I bet you know everyone around here."

"Not everyone," he murmured, "but Akis and I rented an apartment along this waterfront when we started up our business years ago, so we're friends with many of the owners around here."

Vasso started the engine and drove them through the olive groves to the village. An hour later, after they were filled with spinach pie and ouzo lemonade, he carried the last of Zoe's luggage up the stairs to the furnished apartment. The front room window overlooked the horseshoe-shaped harbor. The minute he saw Zoe's expression, he knew she liked the view and the typical blue-and-white décor.

She smiled at him. "This place is really cozy and so colorful. I love it, and it's all mine."

After what she'd recounted earlier about

needing her space, he could believe she was serious. But it bothered him that she was so happy about it.

"I'm glad you like it. Our number-one store is just a few doors down. You can grab breakfast there while you're waiting for the bus."

"If I do too much of that I'm going to get fat, but I want you to know I'm ecstatic to be here," she exclaimed. Vasso couldn't imagine her with a weight problem, not with her beautiful face and body. Her green eyes lifted to his. "Cinderella may have had a fairy godmother, but I've had the perfect godfather who has granted my every wish. Now that your mission has been accomplished, I release you to get back to your life."

Zoe could tease all she wanted, but he sensed she wanted him to leave. The hell of it was he didn't want to go. Since she'd flown to Athens, he'd been a different person and couldn't spend enough hours with her. She was so entertaining he never knew what was going to come out of her mouth next. The thought of her ever being interested in another man disturbed him more than he wanted to admit.

He'd only scratched the surface of her life,

but she'd drawn the line at entering his home. Why? Was it because she didn't trust him after what Chad had done to her? Did she see every man through the filter put there by the other man's defection? Was she afraid of marriage because of that experience?

She didn't bat an eye over renting an apartment with one bedroom. Did that mean she really did like to be alone? He could hear Akis commenting on the subject. *Are you still feeling responsible for her, or is there something more eating at you?*

Vasso had to admit there were a lot of things eating at him. He sucked in his breath. "If you need help of any kind, I'm only as far away as the phone."

"You think I don't know that?" She walked him to the door. "I'm sure we'll see each other again. Hopefully by then Yiannis will have a good word for me."

As Vasso had predicted to Akis, she already had Yiannis eating out of her hand.

"Stay safe, Zoe."

"You, too."

He heard the slight wobble in her voice. It stayed with him as he left the apartment, taking with him the haunting image of her blond hair and sparkling eyes, not to mention the white-on-navy print dress that clung to her figure.

Once he reached the car, he took off for his villa. But he was too upset by emotions churning inside him to stay on the island till morning. If he did that, he'd be tempted to drop by the apartment with some excuse to see her again. Instead he alerted the pilot that he was ready to fly back to Athens.

After the helicopter touched down at the penthouse, he checked any messages his private secretary might have left. Apparently Akis had dealt with everything important. Grabbing a cup of coffee, he went back to his office to dig into the inventories still left to get through. But first he texted his brother.

I'm back in the office working. Zoe Zachos is living in the apartment above Kyria Panos's shop. All is well with Yiannis.

Not two minutes later his brother phoned him back. "Have you contacted Maris?"

"Yes."

"That's good. She phoned several times yesterday wanting to know about you."

"Sorry."

"I get it. So how are things with her?"

"I broke it off with her last night."

"I guess that doesn't surprise me. Whatever happened to 'slow down'?"

Vasso let out a morose laugh. "Look where it got *you.*"

CHAPTER FIVE

August 26

ALREADY IT WAS FRIDAY. Five days without seeing Vasso felt like five years. In the time they'd been together, they'd confided in each other about the very personal things in their lives. He knew information about her she hadn't shared with anyone else. Zoe loved being with him. She ached for his company. He brought excitement into her life.

But she'd better get used to separations because the foundation was only a small part of the huge company he ran with his brother. And the more she heard about their generosity, the greater her need grew to do all she could to help in such a humanitarian effort.

Over the last five days Zoe had been able to introduce herself to every inmate except the twenty-four-year-old guy from Athens named Nestor. The resident therapist was worried about him. He'd been undergoing chemo in the infusion clinic and was in a depressed state, refusing to talk to anyone.

The therapist told her Nestor had been a receptionist at a hotel that went bankrupt. He couldn't find a job and after a few months became homeless. Two months later, he was diagnosed with lymphoma. He usually lived on the steps of a Greek Orthodox Church but spent a lot of time under the nearby bridge with his other homeless friends.

This was the case of another kind priest who got in contact with the center on Paxos and arrangements had been made to get him admitted. Zoe found out that the helicopters owned by the Giannopoulos brothers helped transport patients like Nestor from all over Greece when there was no other solution.

Through Yiannis she learned more about Vasso and Akis. Born to poverty, they'd built a billion-dollar business in such a short period of time it stunned the Greek financial world. That was why the media was always in their face. It explained why Vasso made his home here on Paxos. Evidently his younger brother lived on the nearby island of Anti Paxos.

Just thinking about Vasso caused her breath to catch.

Already she was finding out that the homeless patients were afraid there'd be nothing for them to look forward to once they had to leave the center. That was an area needing to be addressed. Zoe had known the kind of depression that was drawing the life out of Nestor. Now that lunch was over, it would be a good time to visit him.

She took some oranges and plastic forks with her. When she reached his room she found him half lying in a recliner wheelchair. Every room had a sign that said, "Reality is never as dark as the places your brain visits in anticipation." How true.

"Nestor?"

He opened his eyes. They were a warm brown. Despite his bald head, he was good looking, or would be if he were animated.

"If you're too nauseated to talk, I've been there. Mind if I sit down?" She pulled a chair over to him and set the items on the table. "I'm new here. My name's Zoe. I just got out of the hospital in New York City after being there a year. I had lymphoma too."

That brought a spark. "You?"

"I thought I'd be dead by now, but it didn't happen. I also lost my family in a fire, which made things much worse. I understand you don't have family either."

"No. My grandfather raised me, but he died."

"Well we're both very lucky that the Giannopoulos Foundation exists. They've given me a job here. What kind of a job do you want when you leave?"

"I won't be leaving," he murmured.

"Of course you will. As my priest told me, God didn't come to my rescue for nothing. I know how the nausea can make you think you'll never be better. But it will pass. I brought you some things that helped me.

"If you open and smell an orange before you eat, the aroma will make the food tolerable. At least it worked for me. Also, the metal forks and spoons sometimes make you gag. Try eating your food with a plastic fork and see if it makes any difference."

He eyed her with curiosity. Good!

"See you soon. Maybe one of these days

we'll go outside on the patio and have a game of cards. I'll bring a scarf and some snacks. I have an idea you'd make a dashing pirate. You know, young-Zorba-the-Greek style."

She left the room and continued on her rounds until the end of the day. Yiannis wanted her to be his eyes and ears. Besides keeping up on the paperwork, he expected her to make suggestions to improve their services. What was missing? That's what he wanted to know.

Now that she'd been hired full time, they would take turns covering for each other Saturday and Sunday. This coming weekend was his turn to work. Suddenly Zoe had more freedom than she knew what to do with.

When she walked out to catch the bus, the fountain of Apollo was playing. Again she was reminded of Vasso who, like the sun god in his chariot, was so handsome it hurt. She needed to get her mind off him. In the morning she'd take a long hike around the island.

On Sunday, she and Olympia, one of the cooks from the hospital, were going to take the ferry to Corfu from Loggos. While Olympia met with her relatives, Zoe planned to do some sightseeing on her own and was looking forward to it.

A group of workers got on the bus with her. They were already friendly with her and chatted. One by one they got off at different stops. Zoe was the only one who rode all the way into the village. By now the driver named Gus knew her name. Though she might be in Greece rather than New York, there was the same atmosphere of community she'd loved growing up.

When Zoe got off the bus, she headed for one of the *taverna*s that served *mezes* along the harbor front. At twilight the lights from the boats and ferry twinkled in the distance. It was a magical time of night.

Most of the tables outside were taken by tourists, but she finally found an empty one. She'd been anxious to try the various fish appetizers to see how they compared with her mother's cooking. The waiter brought an assortment of octopus, shrimp, sardines, calamari and clams.

Maybe she was biased, but she thought her mom's were better. Then again maybe she was missing her family. How they would have loved to come here for a vacation.

Don't look back, Zoe. You're the luckiest girl in the world to have been given this opportunity. You've been handed a second chance at life. You've been able to realize your dream to work for the Giannopoulos Foundation. You're living in one of the most beautiful spots on earth.

"Such a beautiful young woman sitting alone at the table looking so sad is a sin. Even if it isn't all right, I'm going to join you."

She'd know that distinctive male voice anywhere and looked up in shock. *"Vasso—"*

"Sorrow on a night like this is a tragedy."

Zoe made an odd sound at the sight of him. Tonight he'd dressed in a black silk shirt and tan trousers. Afraid she was staring hungrily at him, she averted her eyes. "I was just doing a little reminiscing about my parents. You caught me at the wrong moment."

He took a seat opposite her at the round table. His nearness did strange things to her equilibrium. "What's on that mind of yours?"

The waiter came, but Vasso only ordered a cup of coffee. She knew he was waiting for an explanation. "I've been sitting here counting my blessings."

"That sounds like you. So you're not missing home then?"

She sat back in the chair. "I stay in touch with my friends through email. As for Chad, he took my advice and is out of my life."

Her heart skipped a beat. "It was the right decision for both of us. Otherwise I wouldn't be sitting here on the island Kyria Panos calls the jewel of the Ionian, eating dinner with my benefactor. If you saw me in a sad mood just now, I was thinking how much my parents would have loved this island and how they longed to visit Florina. But my mother would whisper that these sardines were overly seasoned."

Following his chuckle, he took a sip of the coffee the waiter had brought to the table. "What are your plans for this weekend? I talked to Yiannis and learned it's your turn to be off work until Monday."

She glanced around as if she were afraid to look at him. "We've decided to alternate weekends. The security guards will take turns to cover for us while we sleep there."

"According to him you're turning the place around already."

"Yianni is just being nice."

"So it's Yianni now?" he questioned with a smile.

"The first time I called him that by mistake, he said his wife always dropped the 's' and he ordered me to keep doing the same thing."

"It's clear he's happy with you." Vasso finished his coffee. "How do *you* like your job by now?"

CHAPTER SIX

"I LOVE IT!" Zoe's eyes sparkled like the aquamarine sea around Akis's villa on Anti Paxos. "There's this one patient named Nestor I want to tell you about. But only if you have the time."

"I'm off work for the weekend too. If there isn't something you need to do, why don't we drive to my house to talk? There's a lineup of tourists from the ferry who would appreciate this table."

When she reached in her purse to pay the bill, he checked her movement and pulled out his wallet to do the honors.

"I don't expect you to pay for me."

"Not even when it's your birthday?"

She gasped slightly, but then she shook her head. "Why am I not surprised? You know everything about me."

"Almost everything," he teased. "This one is the big twenty-five. I remember having one of those five years ago."

"Did you celebrate with someone special?"

"If she'd been special, she and I would still be together."

She eyed him frankly. "Your fault or hers?"

"Most definitely mine."

"Don't tell me there hasn't been one woman in your life who meant the world to you?"

He helped her up from the table and they walked along the waterfront to the parking area near the pier. "Her name was Sofia Peri. I asked her to marry me."

After a measured silence, "How long ago?"

"When I was twenty. But the business Akis and I put together hadn't gotten off the ground yet. She needed a man with substance."

Zoe stared up at him before getting in his car. "Just look what *she* missed…"

Touché.

He closed the door and went around to the driver's seat to get in. They drove the short way to his house in companionable silence.

"Where does that road go?" she asked before they reached his villa.

"To the pier where I keep my boat."

She turned to him. "Can we drive down to look at it?"

"If that's what you want." He made a right turn that led to the water's edge where she saw his gleaming cruiser.

There was an enchantment about the night. A fragrant breeze lightly rippled the water. This was Vasso's front yard. "It must be fabulous to go everywhere you want by water. Of course you go by helicopter too, but I can't imagine anything more fun than finding new coasts to explore."

Vasso shut off the engine and turned to her. "I had those same thoughts years ago. When the rich people pulled into our little harbor to eat and buy things from the store where Akis and I worked, I always wondered what that would be like. That was long before it became an Alpha/Omega 24 store."

Her heart ached for how difficult his life had been. "Is that how you met the woman you proposed to? Was she a tourist who came in?"

"No. She lived in the village. We went to

the same church and the same school, even though Akis and I were absent most of the time. Her parents didn't approve of me, but she defied them to be with me."

Zoe felt pained for him. "Was she your childhood sweetheart?"

"You could say that. I assumed we'd get married one day. We were crazy about each other, or so I thought. It helped me get through some difficult times, especially after our father died. Akis and I continued to work there and had saved enough money to buy it from the owner. By then I was nineteen and had to do my military service.

"While I was gone, we wrote to each other and made plans. At least *I* did. But I didn't realize that while I was away, she'd started seeing a local fisherman's son who was making a good living. She never once mentioned him to me until my return. The news that she'd fallen for someone else pretty well cut my heart out."

Zoe didn't know what to say. "My relationship with Chad never got as far as yours." The normal platitudes wouldn't cover it to comfort him because in truth, the woman sounded shallow. If she chose ready money over the true value of Vasso Giannopoulos whom she'd loved for years, then he was well out of it.

"Are you saying you were never intimate with him?"

"No. I was taught to wait for marriage. Guilt kept me from making that mistake. Thank goodness it did since Chad and I weren't meant to be. But I'm truly sorry about Sofia."

"That's past history. Fortunately for me, it was Akis's time to go into the military. I had to do the job of two people to keep our business running. By the time he got back, we went all out to make a success of our lives. Both of us were sick of being looked upon as the impoverished Giannopoulos boys who rarely went to school and had no education. I believe it was harder on Akis, but he's very sensitive about it."

"The poor thing," she said quietly. "Neither of you knew your mother who could have comforted both of you. I can't comprehend it."

"Our father made up for it."

"That's obvious. The two centers you've built in honor of him say everything." Her throat had started to swell. "If I could meet him, I'd tell him he raised the best sons on earth."

"If I keep listening to you, I just might believe it. As long as we're here, would you like to go for a boat ride?"

"I thought you'd never ask," she admitted on a laugh.

"I'll take us on a short drive to the harbor. It's very picturesque at night."

Zoe got out of the car before he could come around to help her and started walking to the boat dock. She turned to him. "What can I do to help?"

His white smile in the semi-darkness sent a rush of warmth through her body. "If you want to undo the rope on this end, I'll take care of the other."

His cruiser looked state-of-the-art, but small enough for one person to manage. She did her part, then stepped in and moved over to the seat opposite the driver's seat. Never in her wildest dreams would she have imagined spending her twenty-fifth birthday driving around an island in the Ionian Sea with a man as incredible as Vasso. If she was dreaming, it didn't matter. She was loving every minute of it.

He stepped in with a male agility that was fascinating to watch and handed her a life jacket to put on. As he started to sit down she said, "You have to wear one too. I'm not the world's greatest swimmer. If I had to save you, it would be kind of scary."

His deep chuckle seemed part of the magic of the night. When they were both buckled up, he started the engine and they went at wakeless speed until they were able to skirt the cove. Zoe got up and stood at the side. Other boats were out, but all you could see were their lights and other lights on the island.

She turned around and braced her back so she could look at Vasso. "I've been thinking about your childhood. Did they offer a class in English when you did go to school?"

He slanted her a glance. "Yes, but we were rarely there. Our major knowledge came from talking to the English-speaking tourists. The owner of the store gave us a book to learn from. Our father told us we had to learn it in order to be successful."

"My parents spoke English and I was lucky

to be taught at school from day one. If I'd had to learn it from a book the way you did and teach myself, it wouldn't have happened, believe me."

"You would if it meant your living."

Her life had been so easy compared to Vasso's, she didn't want to think about it. "I'm sure you're right."

"What kind of books did you read?"

"For pleasure?"

He nodded.

"English was my major, but I have to admit I loved all kinds of literature. In my mind you can't beat the French for turning out some of the great classics. My favorite was Victor Hugo's *Les Misérables* about Jean Valjean, who listened to the priest and did good. One of my classmates preferred Dumas's *Count of Monte Cristo* whose desire for revenge caused him not to listen to the priest."

Vasso slowed the boat because they'd come to the harbor where she could fill her eyes with its beauty. "I've seen the films on both stories. We'll fly to Athens and take in a film one day soon, or we could go dancing if you'd like."

Zoe smiled. "That sounds fun, but finding the time might be difficult." *Don't torture me with future plans, Vasso.* "I have my work cut out here."

In that quiet moment Vasso reached out and caressed her cheek with his free hand. His touch sent trickles of delight through her nervous system. "Yiannis has been thanking me for dropping you on his doorstep. I do believe everyone is happy." In the moonlight his heart-melting features and beautiful olive skin stood out in relief. "Shall we go back to the house?"

More than anything in the world Zoe wanted to see his home, but there were reasons why she had to turn him down. He was her employer, but there was much more to it than that. She'd found herself thinking about him all week, wishing he'd come by the hospital. For her to be looking for him all the hours of the day and evening meant he'd become too important to her already.

She could feel her attraction to him growing to the point she found him irresistible. This shouldn't be happening. If she fell in with his wishes, she could be making the worst mistake of her life. And it would be a big one, because there was no future in it.

"I'd better not, but thank you anyway. This has been a thrill to come out in your cruiser. I've loved every second of it, but I've got a big day planned tomorrow and need to get to bed."

The oncologist had told her that because of her type of lymphoma, the odds according to the Follicular Lymphoma International Prognostic Index indicated she'd live five years, maybe more. No one could guess when there'd be a recurrence.

With that in mind, she needed to keep her relationship with Vasso professional. She was already having trouble separating the line between friendship and something else. By touching her cheek just now he'd stoked her desire for him. He'd mattered too much to her from the beginning and her longing for him was getting stronger.

Whatever the statistics said, Zoe was a ticking time bomb. The breakup with Chad had been hard enough to deal with. But knowing the disease would come back had made her fear another romantic involvement. The only thing to do was stay away from any sign of emotional attachment that could hurt her or anyone else. Zoe had her work at the center and would give it her all.

On their way back to the car she hoped she hadn't offended him. He'd been so kind to find her at the *taverna* and help her celebrate her birthday. Yet once again she felt tension emanating from him, stronger than before.

When he helped her in the car he said, "Tomorrow I'm planning to look at a new property. I'd like you to fly there with me. It'll be a chance for you to see another part of Greece. We'll only be gone part of the day. Once we're back, you can get on with your other plans."

The blood pounded in her ears. "That wouldn't be a good id—"

"Humor me in this, *thespinis*," he cut her off. "Since I came empty-handed this evening, let it be my birthday present to you."

She averted her eyes. "Did Yianni put you up to this?"

"No. I actually thought it up all by myself." On that note she laughed and he joined in. "I like it when you laugh."

Zoe didn't dare tell him how his laugh affected her…the way his black eyes smiled, the way he threw his head back, the way his voice rumbled clear through to her insides making them quiver. Oh no. She couldn't tell this beautiful Greek god things like that.

Her resistance to him was pitiful. "How soon did you want to leave?"

"I'll come by your apartment at eight-thirty."

If he was going on business, then she needed to dress for the occasion. When he went out in public he was targeted by the paparazzi. She wanted to look her best for him.

"What's on your mind?" he asked when he pulled up in back of the apartment.

"Things that would bore a man."

"Try me," he challenged with fire in his eyes.

"What lipstick should I put on, what shoes to match my dress, what handbag will be better. Decisions, decisions. See what I mean?"

He scrutinized her for a moment. "I see a lovely woman. What she wears doesn't matter."

"I'm a fake. If you saw me without my hair you'd have a heart attack." She'd said it intentionally to remind him who she was, and got out of the car. "Someday I'll lose it all again when I have to undergo another session of chemo, so I'll enjoy this momentary reprieve while I can. Thank you for this unexpected evening. I'll be waiting for you in the morning. Good night, Vasso."

She let herself in the back door, but was so out of breath it took a minute before she could climb the stairs. Even if her fairy godfather hadn't needed the reminder, *she* did.

Tomorrow has to be your last time with him, Zoe. Absolutely your last.

After a shower and shave, Vasso put on tan trousers and a silky, claret-colored sport shirt. While he fixed himself his morning cup of coffee, his phone rang. It was his brother.

He picked up. "*Yassou,* Akis."

"Where are you?"

"At the house."

"Good. Raina and I were hoping you'd come over this morning and have breakfast with us. We haven't seen you in two weeks."

"Thanks, but I'll have to take a rain check on that."

After a pause, "What's going on?"

"I'm off on business in a few minutes."

"We already closed the deal on the store in Halkidiki."

He rubbed the back of his neck. "This is something different."

"Then it has to involve Zoe Zachos. Talk to me."

Vasso let out a frustrated sigh. "I've been helping her settle in."

"And that includes taking her on a business trip?" His incredulity rang out loud and clear.

Vasso checked his watch. "I'm going to be late picking her up. I'll explain everything later. Give Raina my love."

The question Akis was really asking went to the core of him. But he couldn't talk about it. Once they got into a conversation, his brother would dig and dig. Zoe had said the same thing about him. They weren't brothers for nothing, and Akis wouldn't stop until he'd gotten to the bare bones. Vasso wasn't ready to go through that. Not yet...

Pieces of last night's conversation with Zoe had shaken him.

I'm a fake. If you saw me without my hair you'd have a heart attack. Someday I'll lose it all again, so I'll enjoy this momentary reprieve while I can.

Chilled by the possibility of the lymphoma

recurring, Vasso started the car and drove to her apartment, unaware of the passing scenery.

When Chad heard I'd been told my disease would probably be terminal, he couldn't handle it. I told him I didn't want him to have to handle it and begged him to take the job offer in Boston and not look back. He took my advice.

Chad's pain would have been excruciating to realize he might lose her. But Zoe had to have been in anguish over so many losses.

Vasso's thoughts flew to his father when he'd been on the verge of death. The sorrow in his eyes that he wouldn't be able to see his sons grow to maturity—the pain that they'd never known their mother—the hope that they would never forget what a wonderful woman and mother she'd been—

Tears smarted his eyes. Not so much for the pain in his past, but for Zoe who didn't know what the future would bring. Their light conversations only skimmed the surface of what went on underneath. Her declaration that she never planned to marry was part of the babble to cover up what was going on deep inside of her.

All of a sudden he heard a tap on the window and turned his head. It was Zoe! He hadn't realized he'd pulled to a stop outside the apartment door. She looked gorgeous in a simple black linen dress with cap sleeves and a crew neck. The sun brought out the gold highlights in her hair.

He leaned across the seat to let her in. She climbed in on those well-shaped legs and brought the smell of strawberries inside. Her lips wore the same color and cried out to be kissed. Her eyes met his. "*Kalimera,* Vasso."

"It's a beautiful morning now, *thespinis.* Forgive me for staring. You look fabulous."

Color rose into her cheeks. "Thank you. After getting caught off guard by the paparazzi in Athens, I thought I'd better be prepared to be seen in the company of one of Greece's major financial tycoons."

Vasso took a deep breath. "I hope that's not the case today. Have you eaten breakfast?"

"Oh yes. Have you?"

"Just coffee."

Her brows met in a delicate frown. "That's all you had last night."

Zoe managed to notice everything. He liked it. He liked her. *So much in fact he couldn't think about anything else.* "I'm saving up for lunch," he said and drove the car back along the tree-lined road to his house where the helicopter was waiting.

"Where are we going?"

"I've decided to let it be a surprise. You'll know when we land at the heliport."

Before long they'd climbed aboard the helicopter and lifted off. Vasso put on his sunglasses and turned on the mic. When he looked over his shoulder he saw that Zoe had put on sunglasses too. She was beautiful and could easily be a famous celebrity. But he was glad no one knew about her. He liked the idea of keeping his find to himself.

He gave her a geography lesson as they flew northward to Macedonia. She knew more Greek history than most people of his acquaintance. Once they neared the desired destination, the land became more mountainous. He could tell her eyes were riveted on the dark green landscape that opened up to half a dozen magnificent lakes. Further on a sprawling city appeared. The pilot took them down and landed in a special area of the airport. When the rotors stopped whirling Vasso said, "Welcome to Florina, Zoe."

She looked at him in wonder. "Are you serious?"

"When you told me your parents had wanted to bring you here for your graduation, it gave me the idea."

"So you don't really have business here?" she asked in a softer voice.

"I didn't say that."

Zoe shook her head and took off her sunglasses. "You do too much for me, Vasso."

"I'd hoped for a better reaction than a lecture."

"I didn't mean to sound like that. Forgive me."

"Come on. I have a limo waiting to take us sightseeing." He got out first then helped her down. The urge to crush her warm body in his arms was overwhelming, but he held back.

The limo was parked nearby. He helped her inside, but this time he sat next to her. "I've asked the driver to take us on a small tour. When I told him your great-grandparents lived here until the outbreak of the Greek Civil War, he promised to show us some of the historical parts of Florina and narrate for us over the mic."

She looked out the window. "I can't believe this is happening."

"I'm excited about it, too. I've never spent time in this area and am looking forward to it."

"Thank you from the bottom of my heart," came her whisper. When he least expected it, Zoe put a hand over his and squeezed it for second. But as she tried to remove it, he threaded his fingers through hers and held on to it.

"I think I'm almost as excited as you are. The cycle of the Zachos family has come full circle today. Seventy years ago your ancestors left this town to get away from communism. Now their great-granddaughter is back to put down her roots in a free society. That's no small thing."

"Oh, Vasso."

In the next instant she pressed her head against his arm. While the driver began his narration—unaware of what was going on in the rear—Vasso felt her sobs though she didn't make a sound. Without conscious thought he put his arms around her and hugged her to him, absorbing the heaves of her body. He could only imagine the myriad of emotions welling up inside her.

After a few minutes she lifted her head and faced straight ahead. "I hope the driver can't see us. Here he's going out of his way to tell us about the city, and I'm convulsed."

"He knows this tour has more meaning for you than most tourists so he'll understand."

"You always know the right thing to say."

For the next half hour the driver took them past buildings and landmarks made famous by the prominent filmmaker Theo Angelopoulos.

"Since the last war I don't imagine the homes my great-grandparents left are even standing," she confided.

"Probably not." Vasso asked the driver to drop them off at a point along the Sakoulevas River. "Let's get out and walk to Ioannou Arti Street so you can get a better view of the twentieth-century buildings along here. There's an archaeological museum we can visit."

She climbed out and put her arm through his as they played tourist. It felt so natural with her holding on to him like this. He could wish this day would go on forever.

"This is fabulous, Vasso. I had no idea the city was so beautiful. To think maybe my great-grandparents walked along this very river."

"Maybe it was along here they fell in love."

Zoe looked up at him in surprise. "I had no idea you're such a romantic at heart."

"Maybe that's because you bring it out in me." Obeying an impulse, he lowered his mouth and kissed those lips he'd been dying to taste. It only lasted a moment, but the contact sent a bolt of desire through him. She broke the kiss and looked away before they walked on.

The limo met them at the next street and they got back in. "If you've had enough, I'll tell the driver to run us by a market the Realtor told me was for sale. He tells me there's a *taverna* nearby where we can try out *burek*. We'll see if it compares to your mother's recipe."

"I'd love that."

Vasso alerted the driver and soon they pulled up in front of a store selling produce. He got out and helped Zoe down. Together they walked inside the busy market. The city was certainly big enough to support one of their stores. But he was curious to know the figures and approached the owner.

"While I talk to him, take a look around and see if there's something you want to buy to take back to the apartment."

She smiled. "Take as long as you need."

Zoe strolled around, eyeing the fruits and vegetables brought in by local farmers. Vasso noticed the customers eyeing her, even the owner who could hardly concentrate when asked a simple question.

When Vasso had learned what he wanted to know, he went in search of Zoe and found her at the back of the market buying a bag of vegetables.

"Don't they sell peppers in Loggos?"

Her face lit up. "No. These are sweet Florina red peppers. My mother remembered her mother and grandmother cooking these. They aren't like any other peppers in the world. I have the recipe. When we get back to Loggos, I'll cook some for you with feta cheese and we'll see if they live up to their reputation. The eggplant looks good, too."

His pulse raced at the thought of going back to Zoe's apartment. "Then let's grab a slice of *burek* at the *taverna* two doors down now, and eat a big meal this evening."

"That sounds perfect."

She hadn't said no. Their day out wasn't going to end the second they flew back to Loggos. That was all he cared about.

After telling the owner he'd be in touch with the Realtor, Vasso carried her bag of precious peppers and eggplant as they walked along the pavement to the outdoor café. He ordered *burek* and Skopsko beer for both of them.

When she'd eaten a bite, he asked for her opinion.

"I'm more curious to know what you think, but you have to tell the truth. If you like it better than mine, it won't hurt my feelings very much."

He burst into laughter and ate a mouthful of the pie. Then he ate a few more bites to keep her in suspense. She was waiting for an answer. Those green eyes concentrated solely on him, melting him to the chair. "It's good. Very good. Yours is better, but I can't define why it's different."

She leaned forward. "You mean it?"

Good heavens, she was beautiful. "I don't

lie, *thespinis*. Let's drink to it." They touched glasses, but she only drank a little bit of hers while Vasso drained the whole thing. Food had never tasted so good, but that was because he was with her and was filled with the taste of her. He wanted more and suspected she did too otherwise she wouldn't be talking about their spending the rest of the day together back on Loggos.

"Excuse me while I freshen up before we leave."

Two hours later they arrived back at Zoe's apartment. While she got busy preparing the peppers, Vasso followed her directions for *moussaka*. "I'm glad you're staying for dinner, Vasso. There's something important I want to talk to you about."

Vasso darted her a piercing glance. His heart failed him to think she had an agenda. Was that the reason he'd made it over her doorstep tonight, and not because she couldn't bear to say good-night to him?

"What is it?"

CHAPTER SEVEN

"I DIDN'T FINISH telling you about one of the patients named Nestor. The poor thing doesn't think he's going to get better. He's depressed, but it isn't just because he's undergoing chemo. He lives with the fear that because he was homeless when he was brought in, he has no work to go back to even if he does recover.

"I've discovered that several of the older patients are afraid they won't get their jobs back if their disease goes into remission. So I was thinking maybe in my off hours I could set up a service to help those patients find a job."

"A service?" One dark brow lifted. "Have you discussed this with Yiannis?"

"Oh no. This would be something I'd do on my own. But I wanted to see what you thought about it."

He put the *moussaka* in the oven. "It's a very worthy project. Maybe even a tough one, but you're free to do whatever you want in your spare time. Surely you know that."

"So you wouldn't disapprove?"

Vasso frowned. "Why would you even ask that question?"

She carefully peeled the skins off the roasted peppers. "Because the people I approach will ask what I do for a living and your foundation will come up. You're a modest man. I don't want to do anything you wouldn't like."

He lounged against the counter while she prepared the peppers to cook with olive oil, feta cheese and garlic. "You couldn't do anything I wouldn't like."

Her gaze shot to his. His compelling mouth was only inches away. She could hardly breathe with him this close to her in the tiny kitchen. "You shouldn't have said that. I'm full of flaws."

His lazy smile gave her heart a workout. "Shall we compare?"

"You don't have any!"

"Then I'll have to break down and reveal a big one."

"Which is?"

"This!" He brushed her mouth with his lips. "When a beautiful woman is standing this close to me, I can't resist getting closer." He kissed her again, more warmly this time.

"Vasso—" She blushed.

"I told you I had a flaw."

She turned from him to put the peppers in the oven. When she stood up, he was right there so she couldn't move unless he stepped away. "I'd like to spend the day with you tomorrow. We'll tour the island and go swimming on a beach with fascinating seashells. What do you say?"

He could probably hear her heart pounding. She'd promised herself that after today, she wouldn't see him again unless it was for professional reasons. Thank heaven she had a legitimate excuse to turn him down.

"Thank you, Vasso. That's very sweet of you, but I can't. I'm going to Corfu in the morning with Olympia."

Those black eyes traveled over her features as if gauging her veracity. "I might have known you'd strike up a friendship with her. She worked in the food services industry before coming to us."

Zoe nodded. "We have that and more in common."

He took a deep breath and moved away. "I'm sad for me, but glad for you to be making friends so fast."

"I found out she bikes with her husband. So they're going to lend me one of their bikes and we'll take rides around the island after work and on our free weekends." She'd added that to let him know her calendar was full.

Another long silence followed, forcing her to keep talking. "Everyone here has been so friendly. I already feel at home here. After moving heaven and earth for me, your job is done. You don't have to worry about me anymore."

Still no response. Needing to do something physical, she set the little breakfast table. After making coffee, she invited him to sit down while she served him dinner. When he still didn't say anything, she rushed to fill the void.

"I'll never forget the gift you gave me today. Seeing the city of my ancestors meant more to me than you will ever know."

"It was a memorable day for me, too," he

murmured. "I want to spend more days like this with you, Zoe. I'd love to go biking with you."

"Between our busy schedules, that could prove difficult." She put the *moussaka* on the table and stood at his side to serve him a plate of peppers. "Tell me what you think about Florina's most famous vegetable."

He took one bite then another and another and just kept nodding.

That was the moment Zoe knew she was in love with him. The kind you never recovered from. To her despair, the thing she hadn't wanted to happen *had* happened. She adored him, pure and simple. His kisses made her hunger for so much more. His touch turned her inside out with longings she wanted and needed to satisfy. *Oh, Vasso... What am I going to do about you?*

Before Zoe blurted that she loved him, she sat down and ate with him. "Um... These really are good."

"You're a fabulous cook, and I've never tasted better *moussaka*."

"You put it together, so you get the credit."

After Vasso drank his coffee, he flashed

her a glance. "The next time we're together, I'll cook dinner for you at my house and I won't take no for an answer."

Zoe let the comment slide. The way he made her feel was toppling her resistance. As she got up to clear the table her cell rang. She reached for her phone lying on the counter.

"Go ahead and answer it," he urged her when she didn't click on.

She shook her head. "It's Kyria Themis. I'll call her back after you leave."

"Maybe it's important, so I'll go."

Much as she was dying for him to stay, she knew this was for the best. Their friendship needed to remain a friendship, nothing more. The kiss he'd given her today had rocked her world. That's why the less they saw of each other, the better.

She walked him to the door. "Good night then, Vasso. This day was unforgettable."

So are you, Zoe.

Vasso got out of there before he broke every rule and started to make love to her. In his gut he knew she wanted him, too. Desire wasn't something you could hide. Whether in the limo or the car, the chemistry between them had electrified him.

Though he didn't doubt she'd already made plans for tomorrow, he sensed she was deliberately trying to keep their relationship platonic. But it wasn't working. Despite her determination not to go to his house, she'd invited him to the apartment tonight and had cooked dinner for him.

There were signs that she was having trouble being too close to him. He'd noticed the little nerve throbbing at the base of her throat before he'd moved out of her way in the kitchen.

While she'd stood next to him to serve dinner, he'd felt the warmth from her body. It had taken all his willpower not to reach around and pull her onto his lap. She was driving him crazy without trying.

On the drive to his house he made a decision to stay away for a few days and let her miss him. He had no doubts it would be harder on him, but work would help him put things in perspective.

Tomorrow he'd do a tour of the stores where he needed to meet with the new store managers to make certain they were following procedure. That would take him the good part of a week. In the meantime Akis would be free to meet with their food distributors in Athens for the critical monthly orders.

Once he was home he phoned his brother to tell him his plans. Before hanging up he said, "I met with the owner of a produce market in Florina today who wants to sell. The Realtor has named a figure that's too high. I think I can get the asking price down, but wanted to know your feelings about us putting up a store there."

"I always trust your judgment, but why Florina? What were you doing there?"

He gripped the phone tighter. "I flew Zoe there for her birthday. Her great-grandparents emigrated from there to America in the mid-forties. Before her parents could take her there for a college graduation present, they died in the fire."

His brother was quiet for a minute. "*Vasso—*"

"I know what you're going to say."

"Since you've already disregarded my warning to take it slow, I was only going to ask if there's a boyfriend in the picture."

"He bailed on her when he found out her disease would probably be terminal."

"That, on top of all her pain," his brother murmured in commiseration. "It would have taken a committed man."

He exhaled sharply. No one knew that better than Vasso. If Chad had loved her enough, he wouldn't have let her talk him into walking away. He could say the same for Sofia who hadn't had the patience to wait until things got financially better for him. Today he rejoiced that he and Zoe were still single.

"How is she working out with Yiannis?"

"They're trading off weekends and he lets her call him Yianni. That's how well they've hit it off. Let me tell you about her latest idea."

After he'd explained, Akis said, "I must admit a job referral service for the patients is a brilliant idea. When are Raina and I going to meet her?"

"I was hoping next Friday evening before she has to go on duty for the entire weekend."

"Do you want to bring her to our house?"

"I fear that's the only way it will work. She isn't comfortable coming to mine yet."

"Then you *have* heeded my warning to a certain extent."

Akis couldn't be more wrong. "Let's just

say that for now I'm letting her set the pace. But I don't know how much longer I can hold out."

"Before you do what?"

"Don't ask that question yet because I can't answer it. All I know is I like being with her." *That was the understatement of all time.* "I'll talk to you later in the week. *Kalinihta.*" He clicked off and got ready for bed.

Once he slid under the covers, Akis's probing question wouldn't leave him alone. Until Vasso knew what Zoe really wanted, he couldn't plan on anything. She'd been hurt by Chad who hadn't seen her through her life-changing ordeal. To have a relationship with Zoe meant earning her trust. He'd begin his pursuit of her and keep at it until she had to know what she meant to him.

After a restless night, he flew to his first destination in Edessa and emailed her to let her know what he'd been doing. He did the same thing every night. By the time Friday came, he couldn't get back to Paxos soon enough. Before he drove to the center, he stopped by the number-one store to check in with the managers and buy some flowers.

"Vasso?" a female voice spoke behind him. He turned around. "Sofia."

Her brown eyes searched his before looking at the flowers. "I was hoping to see you in here one of these days. Can we go somewhere private to talk?"

After she'd turned down his marriage proposal, there'd been times in the past when he would have given anything to hear her say that she'd changed her mind and wanted to marry him. How odd that he could look at her now and feel absolutely nothing. Meeting Zoe had finally laid Sofia's ghost to rest.

"Why not right here? I'm on my way to the center, but I can spare a few minutes. How are you?"

"Not good. I've left Drako."

Somehow that wasn't a surprise to him, yet it brought him no pleasure. Akis had told him he'd seen her in town a few months ago and she'd asked about Vasso. "I'm sorry for both of you."

Her eyes filled with tears. "Our marriage never took and you know the reason why. It was because of you. I've never stopped loving you, Vasso."

He shook his head. "I think if you look deep inside, you'll realize you were young and ambitious. Drako was already doing an impressive fishing business."

"I was a fool."

"I'm sorry for both of you."

"All this time and you've never married. I know it was because of me, and I was hop—"

"Sofia," he cut her off. "I moved on a long time ago."

"Are those flowers for someone you care about now?"

"They're for the woman I love," he answered honestly. Her face blanched. "You have children, and they need you more than ever. Now if you'll excuse me, I have to get to the center. I wish you the best."

He waved goodbye to the owners and hurried out to the car needing to see Zoe. By the time he reached the center he was close to breathless with anticipation. But first he went by Yiannis's office to let him know he was there. The older man told him she was out on the patio with several of the patients.

"When you have the time, I'll tell you about all the changes she's made around here for the better. We're lucky to have her, Vasso."

"I agree. Will it be all right with you if I steal her away for an early dinner?"

"Of course."

"Good."

Without wasting another second he hurried down the hall to find a container for the flowers, then he headed for the doors leading to the patio. She'd arranged four round umbrella tables to be close together with two patients at each one in their recliner wheelchairs. One man and one woman to a table. All wore some kind of head covering and all were playing cards. Zoe was obviously running the show using a regular chair.

She hadn't seen him yet. He stood watching in fascination for a few minutes.

All of them had to be in their late forties or were older, except for one man who looked to be in his twenties. He wore a red paisley scarf over his head like a pirate. As Vasso moved closer, he could tell the younger man was fixated on Zoe. Why wouldn't he be? She was by far the most beautiful and entertaining female Vasso had ever seen. Today she was wearing a soft yellow blouse and skirt.

They were all into the game and the camaraderie between them was apparent. This was Zoe's doing. He reached for a regular chair and took it over to put down next to her. "Can anyone join in?"

He heard her quiet intake of breath when she glanced up at him with those translucent green eyes. "Kyrie Giannopoulos—this *is* a surprise. Please. Sit down and I'll introduce you."

One by one he learned their names. They were profuse in their thanks for his generosity. "We're having a round-robin that's timed," Zoe explained. "Nestor here is on a winning streak." She smiled at the younger man.

"Then don't let me interrupt," he whispered, tamping down his jealousy. "I'll just sit here and watch. Maybe later you'll tell me why the emails you sent back to me were so brief."

For a moment their eyes met. He saw concern in hers. Before the night was out, they were going to talk.

It appeared Nestor couldn't take his eyes off her. When he could see that Vasso wasn't about to leave, the younger man glared at him beneath veiled eyes. The fact that he was recovering after chemo didn't stop the way he studied her face and figure. Was Zoe interested in him?

Vasso couldn't prevent another stab of jealousy, but when he thought about it that was absurd. If there was a bond between them, it had to do with the fact that both Nestor and Zoe had their illness in common. They had an understanding that drew them together. If she suspected the younger man's infatuation, she didn't let it show.

Soon a couple of the nurses came out to take the patients back to their rooms. But Nestor declined help and wheeled his chair out of the room.

"Don't forget movie night tonight!" she called to them. "I'm bringing a treat!"

"We won't forget!" said one of the older men.

Vasso watched her clear up the cards. She was nervous of him. Did he dare believe that she was equally thrilled to see him, and that's why she'd been caught off guard? He desperately wanted to believe she was in love with him, too.

"What's this about movie night?"

She nodded. "During my chemo, there were nights when I couldn't sleep and wished there were something to do. I asked Yianni about it and he told me to organize it. Anything that could increase everyone's comfort was worth it."

Zoe never ceased to amaze him. "You're already revolutionizing this place. What time is your movie night?"

"After nine-thirty. That's when the demons come."

He didn't want to think about the demons she'd lived through. "In that case I'd like you to have an early dinner with me first. Please don't turn me down. My brother and his wife want to meet the new assistant manager. They've invited us over. Maybe you can get Raina to unload about Akis's imperfections. Maybe he pecks at her, too."

She laughed, causing her nervousness to disappear for the moment. "As if I'd ask her a question like that!" There was green fire in her eyes. "I'll have to let Yianni know I'm leaving for a while."

"I've already asked if it's all right, but if you'd rather not leave the center, just tell me.

We can arrange dinner with them for another time."

"No." She shook her head. "That sounds lovely. I've wanted the opportunity to thank Akis. How soon do you want to leave?"

"As soon as you're ready. We'll leave from the hospital roof."

"Let me just freshen up and then I'll meet you at the private elevator in ten minutes."

"Before you go, these are for you." He handed her the flowers.

"Umm. Pink roses. They smell divine."

"They smell like you. I noticed the scent the first time you climbed in the limo."

Color filled her cheeks. "Thank you, Vasso. They're beautiful."

"Almost as beautiful as you."

She averted her eyes. "You shouldn't say things like that to me."

"Not even if I want to?"

"I'll just run to my desk and put them on the counter, then I'll join you."

He could have no idea how much the flowers meant to her. She loved him… Too many more moments like this and all her efforts to keep distance between them would go up in smoke.

After receiving his newsy emails all week, to be given these flowers had her heart brimming over with love for him. It was clear he wasn't about to go away, and now he was whisking her off to his brother's villa.

She was filled with wonder as the helicopter flew over the tiny island next to Paxos. Vasso pointed out the vineyards on Anti Paxos. "If you notice the surrounding water, it's Caribbean green. Your eyes are that color, Zoe."

Every comment from him was so personal it made it harder for her to keep pushing him away. *That's because you don't want to, Zoe. You're in love and you know it.*

As they descended to a landing pad, she could see that the water *was* green, not blue, putting her in mind of emerald isles she'd never seen except in film. Vasso helped her down and kept a hand on the back of her waist as they made their way toward the small stone villa.

"Look at these flowers!" Zoe exclaimed. "It's breathtaking." They lined the mosaic stone pathway.

"Vasso?" she heard a female voice call out.

"Nobody else!" he called back.

In the next instant Zoe caught sight of the lovely American woman who'd married the other Giannopoulos son. She was a blonde, too. Zoe's first impression was that she glowed with health. Vasso had told her they were expecting a baby.

"Zoe? This is my favorite sister-in-law Raina."

"Your only one," she broke into English, rolling her violet eyes. "I'm so glad you could make it." Raina shook her hand before hugging Vasso. "Akis just got back from Athens and will join us after he gets dressed. Please come in. We've been excited to meet you."

Zoe followed her into the most amazing living room. A fireplace had been built in a wall carved out of rock. Between the vaulted ceiling and arches, the stone villa reminded her of pictures from the old family photos that had gone up in flames. The curtains and pillows added marvelous colors of blue and yellow to the décor. Zoe loved it.

"While Vasso goes to find Akis, come out on the terrace, Zoe, and have some lemonade with me."

They walked past the open French doors where the terrace overlooked a kidney-shaped swimming pool. Glorious shades of red, purple and yellow flowers grew in a cluster at one end. Beyond it the sea shimmered. "You live in paradise, Raina."

Her eyes sparkled with glints of blue and lavender. "Every day I wake up and can't believe any place could be so beautiful."

"I know. When Vasso took me on a helicopter ride, I thought I had to be dreaming."

"May we never wake up." Raina Giannopoulos had a charming manner Zoe found refreshing. "Come and sit. I've wanted to meet you ever since we heard you were coming to Greece to work." She smiled. "Don't get me wrong. I love it here, but I miss talking to another American once in a while. Do you know what I mean?"

Zoe liked her very much already. "I know exactly. It's nice to speak English with you."

"I'm working on my Greek, but it's slow in coming."

"I may be Greek in my DNA," Zoe confided, "but I'm American in my heart."

"I thought I was, too, before I married

Akis. Now the Greek part has climbed in and sits next to it."

Zoe laughed while Raina poured them both a glass of lemonade. "Before the guys come out, may I tell you how much I admire you for handling everything you've been through? My grandfather died of stomach cancer and my grandmother from heart failure. I watched them suffer and can only imagine your agony."

"It's over now."

Raina nodded. "You don't know it, but both brothers have been very touched by your story and are astounded by your desire to pay them back. Their father meant the world to them. Until you came along, I don't think either of them realized what good they've really done."

"I know," Zoe whispered, moved by her admission about her grandparents. Raina had known a lot of pain too. "It's hard for Vasso to accept a compliment. I'm afraid all I do is thank him. I'm sure he's sick of hearing about my gratitude."

"If that were the case, you wouldn't be here now."

"That's the thing. He got me this job so fast

he couldn't know how important that is to me. One day my lymphoma will come back, so I want to do all I can for as long as I can."

She saw a shadow pass over Raina's face, but before anything else was said, two black-haired men with striking features came out on the terrace, dressed in casual trousers and sport shirts.

Zoe stared at Vasso's brother, then turned to his wife. "I didn't realize how closely they resemble each other," she whispered. "I thought Vasso was the only Greek god flying around Greece in a helicopter."

"Do you want to know a secret?" Raina whispered back. "When I first saw Akis on the street in Athens, he seemed to be the incarnation of the god Poseidon come to life from the sea."

"I thought you met at a wedding reception."

"That's true, but we almost bumped into each other first on the street."

Zoe smiled. "And you never recovered."

"Never."

"Would you believe my first thought was that Vasso was the sun god Apollo? The statue in the fountain at the center looks just like him. With a husband like yours, it makes you wonder if you're going to give birth to a gorgeous god or a goddess, doesn't it?" After that comment they both laughed long and hard, cementing their friendship.

The men came closer. "What's so funny, darling?"

While Zoe sat there blushing, Raina smiled up at her husband. "We were discussing the baby's gender."

"What's funny about that?" Vasso wanted to know. His intense gaze had settled on Zoe. She knew he wouldn't let it go without an answer.

"Maybe Raina will give birth to a little Poseidon carrying a trident. That's why we laughed."

A knowing look entered Akis's eyes before he kissed his wife on the cheek. "My choice would be an adorable Aphrodite like her mother."

The two of them were madly in love. Zoe could feel it. She was terribly happy for them and about the baby on the way. Zoe would never know that kind of joy. To get married, let alone have a baby, when she knew her cancer could come back wasn't to be considered.

She could see the hunger in Vasso's eyes when he looked at his brother's family. It was killing Zoe, too, because marriage and babies weren't in the cards for her. They couldn't be.

"Akis, let me introduce you officially to Zoe Zachos. Yiannis tells me he doesn't know how they ever got along without her."

"So I've heard." Akis came around and shook her hand. "Apparently your round-robin card game was a huge hit today. We'll have to lay in some chips to make things more interesting for your future poker games."

"That would be fantastic! Thank you. Before another moment goes by, I have to thank you for allowing me to work at the center. I've been given a second chance at life and will always be indebted to you and Vasso." Zoe fought to hide the tears quivering on the ends of her lashes.

She put up her hands. "I'll only say one more thing. I know you're God-fearing men because of your father's example. Christ said that when you've done it unto the least of these, you've done it unto me. Well, I'm one of the least. It's my joy to give back what I can."

Vasso stared at her for the longest time before Raina told the men to sit while she put on an American dinner California-style in Zoe's honor. Fried chicken, potato salad and deviled eggs along with Raina's Parker House rolls recipe.

Zoe had never enjoyed an evening more. Vasso told them about their trip to Florina and discussed the wisdom of putting in a store there. The time passed so fast she protested inwardly when she looked at her watch and saw that she needed to get back to the center.

Raina walked her out to the helicopter. Zoe smelled a haunting fragrance coming from the flowers. "I've never seen Vasso this animated since I met him. He never used to laugh the way he does now. It must be your effect on him. We'll do this again soon," Raina promised.

No. There couldn't be another time. Zoe wouldn't be able to stand being around these wonderful people again when it hurt so much. "Thank you for making me feel welcome, Raina. I've loved it. Vasso told me how you two met. Apparently Akis was running from the maid of honor at the reception and asked you to dance."

"Did he tell you I'd just sprained my ankle and was on crutches?"

"No."

"I was glad I couldn't dance with him because I didn't want anyone to know I was there. The paparazzi were outside waiting. Chloe's wedding was the event of the summer for the media."

Zoe nodded. "They mobbed Vasso the day we went shopping at the department store in Athens. With them always being in the news, it doesn't surprise me that women are after those two brothers. It's really a funny story about you two. Akis is a lucky man. For your information, you could open up your own restaurant serving the food we ate tonight."

The other woman hugged her. "After I heard from Vasso what a great cook you are, that's a real compliment."

Vasso came from behind and opened the door so she could climb in.

"Thanks again, you two. It was wonderful meeting you."

He followed her in. Once they'd fastened

their seat belts, the rotors whined and they climbed into the twilight sky.

Zoe could see Vasso's profile in the semi-dark. He was a beautiful man who'd taken over her heart without trying. She was prepared to do anything for him. That meant weaning herself away from him. He deserved to meet a woman who had a lifetime ahead to give him love and bear his children.

Because of the foundation, she'd been granted five years, maybe a little more, to live life until her time ran out. But it would be a selfish thing to do if she reached out for love. It would be asking too much to deliberately marry a man and have his baby, knowing she would have to go through another period of illness before leaving them. Zoe refused to do that to any man.

"Zoe? We're back at the hospital." Vasso's low voice brought her back to the present.

She thanked the pilot and got out of the helicopter. When Vasso started toward the elevator with her, she turned to him. "I had a marvelous evening and loved meeting your brother and his wife."

"You and Raina really seemed to hit it off."

"She's terrific. Between you and me, your

brother doesn't have anything to worry about. She's crazy about him. No talk of his pecking at her."

Vasso grinned.

"It's obvious they have a wonderful marriage. Now I need to go inside and set things up. You don't need to come all the way to make sure I'm safe."

His dark brows furrowed. "Why are you pushing me away, Zoe?"

After taking a deep breath, she folded her arms to her waist. "Let's be honest about something. Our relationship has been unique from the beginning. The normal rules don't apply. You've done everything humanly possible to help me relocate to a new life, but I'm acclimatized now. For you to do any more for me will make me more beholden to you than ever. I don't want that."

"What if I want to be with you, and it has nothing to do with anything else?"

Zoe lowered her head. "If that's true, then I'm flattered."

"Flattered," he mouthed the word woodenly. "That's all? So if you never saw me again, it wouldn't matter to you?"

"I didn't say that," she defended in a throbbing voice.

"Then what *did* you say?"

"You're trying to twist my words." She pressed the button that opened the elevator door. When she stepped in, he joined her.

"Why are you running away from me?

"I'm not! I'm supposed to be back at work."

"Work can wait five minutes. I want an answer."

"Vasso—"

"Yes? I'm right here. Why won't you look at me? I lived for your emails, but you didn't open up in them."

Her cheeks felt so hot she thought she must be running a temperature. "Because... I'm afraid."

"Of me?" he bit out, sounding angry.

"No—" She shook her head. "Of course not. It— It's the situation," she stammered.

"If you're afraid I'm going to desert you the way Chad did, then you don't know me at all."

"I never said that."

"But it's what you were thinking. Admit it."

"You've got all this wrong, Vasso."

"Then what are you worrying about?"

"*Us!*" she cried.

"At least you admit there *is* an us," he said in a silky tone. In the next breath he reached for her and slid his hands to her shoulders, drawing her close to his rock-hard body. "You're trembling. If it's not from fear, then it means you know what's happening to us. I'm dying to kiss you again. But this time we're not standing in the middle of Florina for all to see."

She hid her face in his shoulder. "I'd rather you didn't. We'll both be sorry if you do."

"I'll be sorry if we don't. Would you deny me the one thing I've been wanting since we met?"

All this time?

"Help me, Zoe," he begged. "I need you."

His mouth searched for hers until she could no longer hold out. When it closed over hers she moaned. Thrill after thrill charged her body as they began kissing each other. One led to another, each one growing deeper and longer. She was so lost in her desire for him she had no awareness of her surroundings.

Vasso's hands roved over her back and hips, crushing her against him while they strained to get closer. She was so on fire for him it wouldn't surprise her if they went up in flames. This wasn't anything like her response to other men, to Chad. All Vasso had to do was touch her and she was swept away by feelings she'd never thought possible.

"Do you have any idea how much I want you?" His voice sounded ragged. "Tell me now how sorry you are." His mouth sought hers again, filling her with sensation after sensation of rapture. But his question made it through the euphoric haze she was in and brought her back to some semblance of reality.

"Vasso—we can't do this any longer," she half gasped, struggling for breath.

"Of course we can."

"No." She shook her head and backed away from him. "I don't want a complication like this in my life."

"You see me as a complication?" he ground out.

"Yes. A big one. You're my ultimate boss. I'm here because of you. We crossed a line this evening, but if we stop right now, then there's been no harm done. I look upon you as a blessed friend and benefactor. I don't want to think of you in any other light."

His face looked like thunder. "Don't make me out to be something I'm not."

"You know what I mean. I need to be here on my own and work out my life without any more help from you. I don't have to explain to you how much I already love it here. But when Father Debakis asked you to interview me, he had no idea what a kind and generous man you really are or how far you would go for the welfare of another human being."

"You're confusing my human interest in you with the attraction we feel for each other, which is something else altogether. Admit the chemistry has been there from the beginning."

"How can I deny it after the way we kissed each other? But it doesn't change the dynamic that I'm an employee of the Giannopoulos Foundation. It would be better if we remain friends and nothing more. You admit you've had other girlfriends. I'm positive there will be more. When another woman comes into your life who sets off sparks, you'll be able to do something about it without looking back."

His black eyes glittered dangerously. "What about you?"

She threw her head back. "I told you the other day. I'm not interested in romance. I want to make a difference in other people's lives. In ways, Ms. Kallistos had the right idea about me after all."

"What rubbish. You know damn well you don't believe what you're saying. I know you don't, but for some reason I have yet to figure out, you've decided to be cruel."

"Cruel?" Her face heated up. "I'm trying to save both of us a lot of pain."

She heard a sharp intake of breath. "You're so sure we'll end up in pain?"

"I *know* we will."

He shook his dark head. "What do you know that I don't?"

Zoe didn't want to say the words. "Think about it and you'll see that I'm right. There's another Raina out there waiting for you to come along. She won't be an employee and she'll be able to give you all the things you've been longing for in your life. Trust me in this. Your turn is coming, Vasso. You're a dear man and deserve everything life has to offer."

Frown lines darkened his handsome features. "Why do I feel like you're writing my epitaph?"

No, my darling. Not yours. Zoe swallowed hard. "I'm not the woman for you."

A haunted expression entered his eyes. "You're not making sense."

"In time, it will be clear to you. Good night, Kyrie Giannopoulos. From now on that's how I'll address you coming and going from the center."

He pushed the button that took them down to the main floor. "Since I'm your boss, I'll accompany you to the entertainment center to offer help if you need it."

Oh, Vasso…

When they reached the game room, there were twelve patients assembled with several nurses standing by. "We've been waiting for you, Zoe," one of the women called out.

Nestor shot her a glance. "Did you forget the treat?"

"Of course not. It's something we chemo patients enjoyed when I was convalescing at the other center. I'm curious to know if you'll like it. But you have to be patient while it cooks."

"What are you going to pull out of your magic bag now?" Vasso said *sotto voce*.

After their painful conversation, his teasing comment made her smile. She ached with love for him and moved over to the microwave. "See these?" Zoe picked up a packet of popcorn lying on the counter.

"They don't sell this in Greece," Vasso murmured.

"True. I brought a supply in my bag when I flew over."

She put a packet in the microwave and pressed the button. In a few seconds the kernels started to pop. Her eyes met Vasso's as that wonderful smell started to permeate the air. When it stopped, she opened the door and pulled out the filled bag. Taking care, she opened it.

Vasso had first dibs. After eating some, he started nodding and took a handful. He couldn't stop with just one and kept eating and nodding. Zoe knew it was a winner and smiled. "I'll let you keep this bag and I'll do another one."

She started cooking it. "Since you're the bird down in the mine and you're still breathing, they'll be willing to try it."

His burst of rich male laughter warmed her heart.

"You think it'll catch on?" she asked.

"Like wildfire. In fact we'll have to stock these in our stores."

"You'll have to tell your managers to cook a batch to entice the customers."

His black eyes smoldered. "You've enticed *me*, Thespinis Zachos."

The popping stopped, but her heartbeat pounded on. She hurriedly pulled out the bag. Vasso took over and opened it before passing it around to those who were willing to try it.

In a louder voice she said, "The popcorn helped some of us at the other center. But if you're too nauseated, then wait till next Friday night," she urged. "Now I'll turn on the film. It's the one that got the most votes to watch. *The Princess Bride* in Greek."

Everyone started clapping.

Vasso turned off the overhead light and came to stand by her with a lazy smile on his face. "Where did you find that?"

"When I went to Corfu with Olympia. This film is a winner with everyone. Have you seen it?"

"No. Any chance of my cooking another bag while we watch?"

If Vasso was trying to break her down, he was doing a stellar job. Those roses had been her undoing. "You don't have to ask me if you want more popcorn. You're the boss."

CHAPTER EIGHT

EVERYTHING HAD BEEN going fine until Zoe reminded Vasso that she worked for him. But that was okay because he wasn't going to let her get away with ignoring him. She would have to put up with him coming to the center on a regular basis. Little by little he would wear her down until she confessed what was going on inside her.

Throughout the entertaining film, he noticed Nestor watching her rather than the movie. One day the younger man would be better. Since Zoe had voiced her concern, Vasso had been thinking about him. Their company had two thousand and one store managers throughout Greece. On Vasso's say-so, any one of them would take Nestor on as an employee.

When the movie was over and the lights

went on, the nurses started wheeling the patients back to their rooms. Vasso volunteered to take Nestor. He felt Zoe's questioning glance on him while she straightened up the room. He kept on going and soon they'd entered his hospital room where Vasso sat on the chair near the table.

"You didn't have to bring me," Nestor murmured. "Thank you."

"You're welcome. Before I leave, I wanted to discuss something with you. I know you're in the recovery phase of your illness. When you're ready to be released, I'm curious to know where you want to go."

"I was born and raised in Athens."

"But I understand you have no family now."

"No," he said, tight-lipped.

"If you could do anything, what would it be?"

"Anything?" Vasso nodded. "I'd like to go to college, but that would be impossible."

At Nestor's age, Vasso had wanted the same thing, but he and Akis were too busy building their business. There was never the right time. "Maybe not."

The younger man looked shocked.

"There are scholarships available for hard-working people. If I arranged for you to get a job in Athens, you could attend college at night."

Nestor's eyes opened wider. "That would be amazing, but I don't know if I'm going to get well."

"I understand you're better today than you were a week ago. Have faith and we'll talk again when the doctor okays your release."

He left Nestor thinking about it and headed for the private elevator. There was nothing he wanted more than to find Zoe and talk to her. But she needed her sleep so she could be in charge tomorrow and Sunday. The one thing that helped him walk away tonight was knowing she wasn't going anywhere. She loved her job and he would always know where to find her.

For the next week he kept busy coordinating work with Akis and continued to send emails to Zoe. He knew his brother wanted to ask him more questions, but Akis kept silent. That was good because Vasso didn't want to get into a discussion about Zoe. They debated the pros and cons of putting up a store in Florina, but didn't come to a decision. The city wasn't growing as fast as some other areas.

On Friday afternoon he flew back to Paxos. After a shower and shave, he put on casual clothes and headed over to the center. Seven days away had made him hungry for the sight of her. But first he checked in with Yiannis who sang Zoe's praises. "We can be thankful all is well with that young woman."

"Amen to that." He expelled a relieved sigh. "I'm going to go over the books with Kyria Lasko in accounting if you need to find me." Vasso knew he wasn't fooling the admiral, but he appreciated the older man for not prying into his personal life.

Two hours later he walked down the hall. When he couldn't see Zoe at the front desk, he headed for the entertainment center. Friday night was movie night. He had a hunch she was in there setting things up for later. But when he went inside, he only found a couple of patients with a nurse.

"Have you seen Thespinis Zachos?"

"She just left, but she'll be back at nine-thirty."

Vasso thanked her and left the hospital in his car. En route to the town center he phoned her. By the time she picked up, his pulse had jumped off the charts.

"Vasso?"

She sounded surprised. He'd missed her so much just the sound of her voice excited him. "I'm glad you answered. Where are you?"

After a pause, "At the apartment."

"No bike riding today?"

"No. Our plans fell through. Her husband hurt his leg biking, so she's home taking care of him this weekend."

"Sorry to hear that. I flew in earlier and worked with the accountant at the center. I didn't see you anywhere. Have you eaten dinner?"

"Not yet."

"I'd like to talk to you about Nestor. Would you like to meet me at Psara's? I don't know about you but I'm craving fish."

He could hear her thoughts working. "That's the *taverna* down near the parking area?"

"Yes. I'm headed there now if you'd like to join me. But if you have other plans, I'll understand."

"No—" she exclaimed, then said no in a

quieter voice. "Nestor told me you talked to him last week."

"That's right."

"You…planted a seed."

Good. "If you want to discuss it, I'll be watching for you." Without waiting for a response, he clicked off and pulled into the parking. He got out and hurried toward the *taverna* to grab a table before the place filled up. Being that it was a Friday night, the paparazzi were out covering the waterfront. Celebrities from Athens often came to Loggos for dinner. Vasso couldn't escape.

In a few minutes, every male young or old stared at the beautiful blonde woman making her way toward him. She'd dressed in a leaf-green blouse with a white skirt tied at the waist. He experienced the same sense of wonder he'd felt when he'd seen her the first time. She was like a breath of fresh air and walked with a lilt on those fabulous legs.

When Vasso stood up to pull out her chair for her, several journalists caught her on camera. She couldn't have helped but see them. "Ignore them," he muttered. "Pretty soon they'll go away."

"Not as long as you're here." But she said it

with a smile. "I knew I was taking a chance to be seen with you."

"You're a brave woman, but then we already know that about you." His comment brought the color flooding into her cheeks.

The waiter came to pour coffee and take their order. They both chose the catch of the day. Once they were alone again, he studied her classic features. "Thanks for answering my emails. You've kept me abreast of everything going on at the center. But you never share your personal feelings. How *has* your week gone?"

"Every day is different. I couldn't be happier," she said through veiled eyes. "What about yours?"

"I can't complain as you know from my messages to you, but thanks for asking."

Considering what it had been like to get in each other's arms last week, this conversation was a mockery. But he'd play her game for a while longer. "How much did Nestor tell you?"

Now that he'd changed the subject to something important to her, she grew animated. "He mentioned that you talked to him about a scholarship so he could go to night school. He's been in disbelief that you really meant it."

Vasso sucked in his breath. "I would never have brought it up if I weren't serious. Earlier this week I talked to the manager of our number-four store in Athens. He'd be willing to give Nestor a job. I have no idea if he would want to work in a convenience store after being employed at a hotel, but—"

"I'm sure he would!" she cried out excitedly. "Oh, Vasso—there's been a light in his eyes that hasn't been there until now. It's because of you."

No. That light had to do with Zoe. She ignited everyone she met. "How much more chemo does he have to go through?"

"He's had his last treatment. The doctor has high hopes for his recovery."

"In that case I'll come to movie night tonight and tell him."

His news made her so happy he realized she couldn't tell him not to come. "Hope will make him get well in a hurry."

The waiter chose that moment to bring their dinner. When he walked away Vasso said, "That's the idea, isn't it. We all need hope."

That little nerve at the base of her throat

was pulsing again. She started to eat her fish. "Between you and Father Debakis, I don't know who will deserve the bigger reward in heaven."

"Your mind is too much on the hereafter," he teased. "I'm quite happy with life right here."

She flushed. "So am I. It's just that I'm so than—"

"Don't say that anymore, Zoe. I'm quite aware of how you feel. I want to talk about how we feel about each other. I can't stay away from you. I don't want to. So we need to talk about where we're going to go from here. I *know* you feel the same way about me."

Her head lifted and their gazes collided. "I admit it, but you'd have to be in my shoes to understand why it wouldn't be a good idea for us to get any more involved."

"I can't accept that."

Zoe's expression sobered. "You're sick of hearing the same thing from me, aren't you?"

If he dared tell her what he really thought, she'd run from him. He couldn't handle that. "I'm not saying another word while we're the focus of other people."

One journalist had stayed longer to get pictures of the two of them. Vasso shot Zoe a glance. "If you're through eating, let's head for my car and ruin that guy's evening."

Her sudden laugh always delighted him. He put money on the table and got up. She was still chuckling when they reached the Lexus and he helped her inside. Zoe looked over at him as he drove. "Even paradise has its serpents."

"They have to earn a living, too."

Her eyes rounded. "You feel sorry for them?"

"No, but I understand that the need to make money in order to survive makes some people desperate enough to take chances."

"You're right, of course. I've never been in that position." She glanced at him. "I've never gone to bed hungry in my life." There was a catch in her voice. "Because of your foundation, I've been taken care of in miraculous ways. Sometimes I'm overwhelmed by your generosity."

Vasso couldn't take it anymore. "Overwhelmed enough to do me a favor?"

"I'd do anything for you. Surely you know that by now."

"Then come to my house after movie night

is over. There's something I have to discuss
with you, but we'll need privacy."

He heard her quick intake of breath. "That
sounds serious."

"It is. Don't tell me no. I couldn't take it."

Zoe trembled, wondering what had happened
to put him in this cryptic mood. If he was
unhappy with some of the innovations she'd
made at the hospital, all he had to do was tell
her up front. Maybe Yianni had confided that
she wasn't working out, but he didn't have the
heart to tell her to her face because he was
such a sweetheart.

When they reached the center, he parked
the car and they entered through the front
door.

She saw the clock. "It's almost time. I need
to hurry to the game room and set up."

"Go ahead. I'll be there in a minute."

Did he want to talk to Yianni again?

Zoe went to the restroom first so she could
pull herself together. She had the idea he
was going to discuss her future here at the
foundation. Could he be going to let her go?
Fear stabbed at her. Maybe coming to work
for him hadn't been a good thing after all.

The passion enveloping them last week had only muddied the water. Tonight things were crystal-clear.

If Father Debakis hadn't intervened, she wouldn't be in this precarious position now. It wasn't his fault, of course. If she hadn't been so desperate to repay her debt, she wouldn't have caused all this trouble.

That's what Vasso had been alluding to earlier. Desperation was responsible for all kinds of mistakes. Her biggest one had been to accept his offer to relocate to Greece and continue taking his charity for the rest of her life.

Of course she was earning a salary now, so she hoped that wasn't what it looked like to him. She buried her face in her hands, not knowing what to think.

She wished her mother were around to talk to her about this. The great irony about that was the fact that if her parents were still alive, Zoe wouldn't be thousands of miles away from home. She'd be finishing college and getting on with her life, never knowing of Vasso's existence. Instead she'd dumped all her problems on Vasso who hadn't asked for them in the first place.

Zoe was terribly conflicted. She'd acted besotted in his arms, but as he'd reminded her, the emails she sent back to him didn't say anything about her feelings. In her heart she'd been watching for signs of him all week. When he hadn't come to the center before tonight, she was desolate. But she couldn't have it both ways, not when she'd told him she wanted to keep their relationship professional.

What a laugh she must have given him. No doubt he saw her as the worst kind of needy female. If she kept this up much longer, he'd be forced to find her something else to do in order to get her out of his hair. But he was such a good man he would never fire her without a new plan.

When she'd washed the tears off her face, she headed for the entertainment center. Eight patients showed up. The other four had just been through another session of chemo and wouldn't rally for a few days.

Vasso had singled out Nestor. While he thrilled him with a job offer, she popped more popcorn and started a movie. This time it was the Greek version of an old film, *Zorba the Greek*. The audience would complain that Anthony Quinn was Mexican, not Greek then they'd pull the crazy plot apart. Hopefully it would entertain them enough for a little while to forget how sick they felt.

By the end of the film, no one wanted the evening to be over. It proved to her that movie night worked. While the nurses took the patients back to their rooms, she tidied the place. But when she followed Vasso out of the center to his car, her heart felt as if it weighed a stone. She dreaded what was coming and her legs felt like dead weights.

On the drive to his house she turned to him. "How did your conversation go with Nestor?"

Vasso let his wrists do the driving. "He sounded just like you when I told him I'd find him an apartment near the number-four store. That way he could walk to work and take the bus to the university after he was released. I don't think he could see the film through the tears."

No. Nestor's gratitude would know no bounds for their benefactor, but she refrained from saying anything because Vasso didn't want to hear it.

Zoe tried to gear up for what was coming. How awful that a conversation with him would take place in his house, the one personal area of his life she'd tried to stay away from. She loved it already just seeing it from the air.

He drove around the back of it. It had been built near the water's edge. They entered a door into the kitchen area with a table and chairs. Though small like a cottage, huge windows opened everything up to turn it into a beach home, making it seem larger. No walls.

Everywhere you looked, you could see the sea. All you had to do was open the sliding doors and you could step out on a deck with several tubs of flowers and loungers. Beyond it, the sand and water were at your feet.

A circular staircase on one side of the room rose to the upper floor. It had to be a loft. The other end of the room contained the rock fireplace with a big comfy couch and chairs.

"Would you like a drink?"

She shook her head. "Nothing, thank you."

"Let's take a walk along the beach. The sand feels like the finest granulated sugar. I do my best thinking out there. We'll slip off our shoes and leave them inside. You can wash your feet later at the side of the deck."

After she did his bidding, she followed him outside. Night had descended. A soft fragrant breeze with the scent of thyme blew at her hair and skirt. She knew it was thyme because there was the same smell at the center. Yianni had explained what it was. He was a walking encyclopedia of knowledge.

She could talk to him the way she did with Father Debakis. The wonderful man had great children who looked after him, but he'd loved his wife to distraction and talked to Zoe about their life together. How heavenly to have enjoyed a marriage like Yianni's.

When they'd walked a ways, Vasso stopped and turned to her. The time had come. Her body broke out in a cold sweat. To her shock, he cupped her face in his hands and lifted it so she had to look at him. Zoe couldn't decipher the expression in his eyes, but his striking male features stood out in the semi-darkness.

"I want to start over."

She blinked. "What do you mean?"

"I mean, I'd like us to do what two people

do who have met and would like to get to know each other better."

After everything she'd been thinking as to what might be the reason why he'd brought her here, Zoe was incredulous. "That's the favor?"

"I know it's a big one. Last week you made it clear you didn't want anything more than friendship from me, but we moved past that after your arrival in Greece. I want to spend this weekend with you and all the weekends you're available from here on out."

The ground shifted.

She was positive she'd misunderstood him.

"Did you hear me?" he asked in an urgent voice.

"You *can't* be serious." She grasped his wrists, but he still cradled her face in his hands.

"Why are you acting like this, Zoe?"

"Because you're carrying your sense of responsibility to me too far."

"Does this feel like responsibility?" He lowered his mouth to hers and kissed her long and hard until she melted against him. Zoe was delirious with desire after being away from him for a whole week. "Tell me the real reason you're fighting me," he said after lifting his head. They were both out of breath. "I know you're attracted to me. You told me there's no one else in your life." The warm breath on her mouth sent a fire licking through her body.

"There isn't, but Vasso—" she moaned his name, "I can't be with you. If I had known this was going to happen, I would have changed my mind and stayed in New York. I would have found another place to work."

His brows met. "You don't mean that. You're lying to cover up what's really wrong."

Making a great effort, she eased herself out of his arms. "You're a very intelligent man. If you think hard about it, you'll know why this won't work. My cancer is in remission, but no one knows when it will come back."

She heard him suck in his breath. "Guess what? Tomorrow I could go down in the helicopter and never be seen again. It could happen. But if I looked at life like that, nothing would get accomplished."

"A possible helicopter crash one day compared to a recurrence of cancer are two different things."

He raked his hands through his hair. "No. They're not. No matter what, life is a risk."

"But some risks are more risky than others, Vasso. To get close to you is like buying something you want on time. One day— much sooner than you had supposed—you'll have no choice but to pay the balance in full. It will be too heavy a price to have to come up with all at once. I won't let you get into that position."

This time his hands slid up her arms. "You honestly believe you're going to die soon? *That's* what this is all about?"

"Yes. But I don't know the timetable and neither do you. What I do know is that you watched your father die of the same disease. No one should have to live through the trauma of that experience a second time in life. You and your brother have fought too hard to come all this way, only for you to get involved with a time bomb, because that's what I am."

He drew her closer. "Zoe—"

"Let me finish, please? I saw the love Akis and his wife share. With a baby on the way they're totally happy. He doesn't have to worry that Raina is going to be stricken by the inevitable.

"Don't you understand? I want you to have the same life *they* have. No clouds on the horizon. To spend time with me makes no sense for you. I'm a liability and I made Chad see that. He was smart and did the right thing for both of us."

Vasso's features darkened. "How was it right for you?" his voice grated.

"Because I would have been more depressed to watch his suffering over me when I could do nothing to alleviate it. Just think about what it felt like when your father was dying, and you'll understand exactly what I'm talking about. It would have been so much harder on me if Chad had been there day and night. I couldn't have handled it."

"I'm not Chad." His hands slid to her shoulders. "Did you love him?"

Vasso's question caught her off guard. "I… thought I did. There are all kinds of love."

"No, Zoe. I'm talking about that overpowering feeling of love for another person that goes so deep into the marrow, you can't breathe without it."

He'd just described her feelings for him

and pulled away before he read the truth in her eyes. "I don't want to talk about this anymore. If it's all right with you, I'd like to go home."

She turned back and hurried toward the deck where she could wash the sand off her feet. By the time he'd caught up to her, she'd gone inside and had slipped on her shoes.

"Before we go anywhere, I need to tell you something important, Zoe. Will you listen?"

They stood in the middle of the room like adversaries. Spiraling emotions had caused her to shake like a leaf. "Of course."

"Something unprecedented happened to me when I flew to New York to interview you. I didn't ask for it, but it happened. I haven't been the same since. Like you with Chad, I thought I loved Sofia. She'd always been there. We'd been a couple for such a long time, it just seemed normal for us to get married.

"Luckily, she got impatient. While I was in the military, she couldn't wait for me. Though I didn't know it at the time, she did me the greatest service in the world because it was apparent she wasn't the one for me.

"After surviving that hurdle, Akis and I led

a bachelor existence for years. When Raina came into his life, it was as much a shock to me as to him. He'd been with other women, but she knocked him sideways without even trying, and transformed his life. I can promise you that if she'd been a recovering cancer patient, it would have made no difference to him."

"That's what you say because it's what you want to believe." She shook her head. "I can see there's no way to get through to you on this."

"You're right. There's only one solution to end our impasse."

"Exactly. By ending it now."

"I have a better idea in mind."

Zoe couldn't take much more. "I need to get back to the apartment."

"I'll take you, but I want you to think very seriously about my next words."

She reached for her purse and started for the kitchen. "Will you tell me in the car?"

Without waiting for him, Zoe went outside and walked along the path to his Lexus. Afraid to have contact, she quickly got in and shut the door.

Vasso went around to his side of the car

and started the engine. But before he drove them to the road, he slid his arm along the seat so that his fingers touched the ends of her hair. Immediately her body responded, but she refused to look at him.

"We need to get married."

Her gasp reverberated in the interior. "*Married—*"

"The sooner the better. According to your timetable, we might have five years together before everything comes to an end. I want to give you children. I'd rather take those five years and live them fully with you, than walk away from you now and leave us both in pain."

"I won't be in pain," she defended in a quiet voice while her heart ran away with her at the thought of having his baby.

"Well, I will." He tugged gently on her hair strands. "After the way you kissed me back tonight, I know for a fact you'll be in pain, too. I don't need an answer yet, but I'll look for one soon."

"No—" she whispered in agony. "You mustn't."

"If I'd let the *no*s and the *mustn't*s get in the way, I wouldn't be where I am today.

You and I don't have the usual problems that beset couples. We know who we are and exactly what we're getting into. We've learned how precious life is. We've been made brutally aware that there are no guarantees for the future, only what we're prepared to build together."

She swallowed hard. "What it proves to me is how far you would go to honor the wishes of Father Debakis."

"He has nothing to do with this!"

"Then why would you be willing to make the ultimate sacrifice by marrying me and giving me a home when you know I have a very short life span."

"Because I love you."

"I love you, too, but I wonder if you remember the warning you gave me in New York. You said, 'Be sure it's what you want.' How sad someone didn't warn you to be sure it was what *you* wanted."

"You're putting up a defense because of your own insecurities." He drove the car to the road and they headed for the village.

"Vasso, you don't want to marry me. We're both temporarily attracted to each other. You're like any red-blooded bachelor might be, but you're not in love with me. I refuse to be your personal project.

"I came here to work and pay you back for your generosity. Wouldn't it be a great way to show my gratitude by becoming your wife? Then you'd be forced to take care of me for however long I have left.

"Forget children. No way would I want to leave a baby for you to raise on your own. Your father did that. I won't allow history to repeat itself. You and Akis have been through so much, you deserve all the happiness you can find.

"Sofia Peri didn't know what she was doing when she let the most marvelous man on earth slip through her fingers. If you'd married back then, you'd probably be a father to several darling children. I should never have come here."

Yianni had gotten along fine before Zoe had arrived. The center would run smoothly whether she was there or not. If she flew back to New York, she could get a job as a cook. When she'd saved enough money she could finish her last semester of college. Then she could get a job teaching school and send money to the foundation every month.

It was the best plan she could think of under the circumstances.

When she got back to the apartment, she'd phone Father Debakis and have a heart-to-heart with him. He was probably at dinner and could talk to her when he was through. The priest would understand her dilemma and give her the guidance she needed because heaven help her, she couldn't make this decision without his blessing.

Vasso drove around to the back of the shop. She opened the door before he came to a stop. "Thank you for bringing me home. You made Nestor a happy man tonight."

"And what about you?"

"You already know what I think."

"We're not finished, Zoe."

"How can I convince you that this just won't work?"

"I didn't realize you were so stubborn."

"Then be thankful I'm not the marrying type. You've dodged a bullet. Good night."

CHAPTER NINE

FOR THE NEXT week Vasso worked like a demon, traveling from city to city to check on stores while Akis worked out of the Athens office. After the last conversation with Zoe, he knew she needed time to think about their situation without being pressured.

Now that it was Friday evening, he couldn't stay away any longer and flew to Paxos. She would be on duty this weekend and couldn't run away from him. After they watched a movie with some of the patients, he'd get her alone to talk until he convinced her they belonged together.

At five to six he tapped on Yiannis's half-open door and walked in. Zoe wasn't out in front, but he didn't expect her to be.

He found the admiral pouring himself coffee from a carafe brought in on a cart from the kitchen. The older man was using the cup Zoe had given him. He turned to Vasso. "Ah. You're here at last."

By his sober demeanor Vasso sensed something was wrong. "Did I miss a call from you?"

"No, no." He walked back to his chair. "Sit down so we can talk."

Not liking the sound of that, he preferred to remain standing. Yiannis looked up from his desk. "I have a letter here for you. It's from Zoe. She asked me to give it to you when you came by and not before."

His heart plummeted. He took the envelope from him, almost afraid to ask the next question. "Where is she?"

"She flew back to New York on Tuesday."

The breath froze in his lungs.

"On Sunday she came over, white as a sheet, and submitted her resignation. Zoe's the best assistant I could have asked for, but the tragic expression on her face let me know she's been suffering. She told me she was so homesick she couldn't stay in Greece any longer. The sweet thing thought she could handle being transplanted, but apparently it was too big a leap. Kyria Lasko is helping me out again."

His agony made it hard to talk let alone think. "I'll find a temporary accountant from headquarters until we can find the right person to assist you," he murmured.

"You'd better sit down, Vasso. You've gone quite pale."

He shook his head. "I'll be all right. Forgive me. I've got things to do, but I'll be in touch."

Vasso rushed out of the hospital and drove to the village at record speed. He parked the car and ran along the waterfront to the gift shop. The second Kyria Panos saw him she waved him over with an anxious expression. "If you're looking for Thespinis Zachos, she's left Greece."

He felt like he was bleeding out. "I heard the news when I was at the center earlier. Let me pay her bill."

"No, no. She paid me. Such a lovely person. Never any trouble."

Not until now, Vasso's heart cried out.

He thanked the older woman and drove back to his house. After making a diving leap for the couch he ripped open the envelope to read her letter. She'd only written one short paragraph.

Forgive me for accepting your offer of employment. It has caused you so much unnecessary trouble. I'm desolate over my mistake. One day I'll be able to start paying you back in my own way.

My dear, dear Vasso, be happy.

Blind with pain, he staggered to the storage closet and reached for his bike. He'd known pain two other times in his life. A young teen's loss of a father. Later a young man's loss of his childhood sweetheart. This pain was different.

Zoe thought she could spare him pain by disappearing from his life. But with her gone, he felt as if his soul had died on the spot. Vasso didn't know how he was going to last the night, but he couldn't stay in the house.

He took his bike out the back door and started cycling with no destination in mind. All he wanted to do was keep going until he got rid of the pain. It was near morning when he returned to his house and took himself up to bed.

The next time he had cognizance of his surroundings, he could hear Akis's voice somewhere in the background urging him to wake up. He couldn't figure out where he was. How had he made it upstairs to his bed?

His eyelids opened. "Akis?"

"Stay with me, Vasso. Come on. Wake up."

He groaned with pain. "Zoe left me."

"I know."

"Did you see her letter?"

"That, and your bike lying on the ground at the back door."

He rubbed his face with his hand and felt his beard. "How did you find out?"

"Yiannis called me yesterday worried about you."

"What's today?"

"Sunday."

He opened his eyes again. "You mean I've been out of it since Friday?"

"Afraid so." His brother looked grim. They'd been through every experience together. "You've given me a scare, bro. I was worried you might have driven yourself too hard and wouldn't wake up. Don't ever do that to me again."

Vasso raised himself up on one elbow. "A week ago I asked her to marry me. Friday night she left her answer with Yiannis. I wanted her so badly I pushed too hard."

"It's early days."

"No. She left Greece to spare me. Zoe's convinced the disease will recur."

Akis sighed. "Raina picked up on that the night you came for dinner."

"For her to give up the job she wanted was huge for her. There's no hoping she'll come back."

"Why don't you get up and shower, then we'll fly to my house. Raina has food ready. Once you get a meal in you, we'll talk. Don't tell me no. This is one time you need help, even if you are my big brother."

September 23, Astoria, New York

"Zoe? Come in my office."

She knew what the doctor was going to say and was prepared for the bad news. This was her first checkup since she'd left the hospital six weeks ago. The month she'd spent in Greece was like a blip on a screen, as if that life had been lived by a different person.

She'd decided not to call Father Debakis. No one at the church knew she was back in the US. Zoe prayed Ms. Kallistos hadn't seen her slip in the hospital and would never know about this appointment.

Zoe had made up her mind she wouldn't depend on the charity of others ever again. While she was staying at the YWCA, she'd been going out on temporary jobs to survive. There was always work if you were willing to do it. This was the life that had put Nestor in a depression. She could see why.

If any good had come out of her experience on Paxos, it had been to introduce him to Vasso who had not only saved his life through his charity, but had made it possible for him to go to college.

Vasso... Zoe's heart ached with a love so profound for him she could hardly bear to get up every day and face the world without him.

"Zoe? Did you hear me?"

She lifted her head. "I'm sorry. I guess I was deep in thought."

He frowned. "You've lost five pounds since you were released from the hospital. Why is that?"

"With the recurrence of cancer, that doesn't surprise me."

"What recurrence?"

Zoe shook her head. "You don't need to be

gentle with me, doctor. Just tell me the truth. I can take it.'

He cocked his head. She had to wait a long time before he spoke again. "I'm beginning to think that if I told you the truth, you wouldn't recognize it, let alone believe me. I *am* a doctor, and I've sworn an oath to look after the sick."

"I know," she whispered.

"But you think I'm capable of lying?"

She bit her lip. "Maybe not lying, but since you work with cancer patients, I realize you're trying to be careful how you tell a patient there is a death sentence in the future."

He leaned forward. "We all have a death sentence awaiting us in life. That's part of the plan. In the meantime, part of the plan is to live life to the fullest. Something tells me that's not what you've been doing."

Those were Vasso's words. It sent prickles down her spine.

"There's no recurrence of cancer, Zoe. I'm giving you another clean bill of health."

"Until another six weeks from now, then it will show up."

He made a sound of exasperation. "Maybe

you weren't listening to me the first time I told you this. In people like you with none of the other complicating factors, the statistics prove that about ninety-one out of every one hundred people live for more than five years after they are diagnosed. And seventy-one out of every one hundred people live for more than ten years. Some even live to the natural end of their lives."

She'd heard him the first time, but she hadn't been able to believe it. *Was it really possible?*

"Since you're cancer-free and in perfect physical shape, I want to know the reason for your weight loss. It has to be a man."

She struggled for breath. "You're right."

"Tell me about him."

Zoe had refused to give in to her feelings since returning from Greece. But with the doctor who'd been her friend for a whole year pressing her for an explanation, she couldn't hold back any longer and blurted everything in one go. The tears gushed until she was totally embarrassed.

"Before I see my next patient who's waiting, do you want to know what *I* think, girl?"

Girl? He hadn't called her that in a long

time. Surprised, she looked at him, still needing to wipe the moisture off her face. "What?"

"You're a damn fool if you don't fly back there and tell him yes. I don't want to see you in my office again unless you have a wedding ring on your finger!"

September 25, Athens, Greece

When the ferry headed toward the familiar docking point at Loggos, Zoe was jumping out of her skin with nervous excitement. She'd taken the cheapest one-way night flight from JFK to Corfu and caught the morning ferry to Paxos Island. While on board she changed into walking shorts and sneakers. Everything else she owned was in her new suitcases. Luckily the largest case had wheels, making it easier for her to walk along the waterfront to the gift shop.

Kyria Panos looked shocked and anxious when Zoe entered her store. "I didn't know you were back. If you want the apartment, I've already rented it. I'm sorry."

"Don't be. That's good business for you! I just wondered if I could leave my luggage here. I'll pay you and be back for it by the end of the day."

"You don't have to pay me. Just bring it behind the counter."

"You're so kind. Thank you."

"Did you know Kyrie Giannopoulos tried to pay me for your rental?"

"No, but that doesn't surprise me." There was no one in this world like Vasso. "I'll buy one of these T-shirts." She found the right size and gave her some euros. "Mind if I change in your bathroom?"

"Go ahead. Whatever you want."

Having deposited her luggage and purse, she left and was free to buy her favorite snack of a gyro and fruit at Vasso's number-one store. Once she'd eaten, she rented a bike from the tourist outfit at the other end of the pier and took off for Vasso's beach house.

Though she hadn't lived on Paxos for very long, it felt like home to her now. The softness of the sea air, the fragrance, it all fed her soul that had been hungering for Vasso. Raina had said it best. "I thought I was American too before I married Akis. Now the Greek part has climbed in and sits next to my heart." Zoe could relate very well.

She had no idea if Vasso would be home or not. If she couldn't find him, she'd bike to the center and drop in on Yianni. He was a sweetheart and would be able to help her track him down without giving her presence away. She wanted, needed to surprise Vasso. It was important she see that first look in his eyes. Just imagining the moment made it difficult to breathe.

The ride through the olive groves rejuvenated her. Every so often she'd stop to absorb another view of the azure sea and the white sailboats taking advantage of the light breeze. She removed her helmet to enjoy it. While she was thinking about Vasso, she saw the local bus coming toward her. It slowed down and a smiling Gus leaned out the window.

"*Yassou*, Zoe! Where have you been?"

"In New York, but I'm back to stay!"

"That's good!"

"I agree!"

After he drove on, she put her helmet back on and started pedaling again. She went through alternating cycles of fear and excitement as she contemplated their reunion. Zoe wouldn't allow herself to be bombarded with negative thoughts again. She'd weathered too many of them already. Because of a lack of faith, she'd wasted precious time, time she and Vasso could have had together.

Zoe stopped every so often to catch her breath and take in the glorious scenery. She had no way of knowing if he'd be at the house, but it didn't matter. This was his home. He would return to it at some point, and she'd be waiting for him.

Akis looked at Vasso. "What do you think about him?" The last person they'd interviewed for the assistant's job at the hospital went out to the lounge to wait. Over the last week there'd been a dozen applicants for the job before him.

"I think he's as good as we're going to get."

"His disability won't present a problem and he's ex-military. Yiannis will like that."

Vasso nodded. Neither of them wanted to admit Yiannis had been so unhappy about Zoe's resignation he'd found something wrong with anyone they'd sent for an interview. He'd rather do the extra work himself.

"Will you tell him? I need to get back to the house if only to find out if it's still standing." Since the Sunday Vasso had awakened to a world without Zoe in it, he'd been living at the penthouse when he wasn't out of the city on business. He got up and headed for their private elevator.

"Hey, bro." Akis's concern was written on his face. "Come over for dinner tonight."

"Can I take a rain check?" Akis and Raina had done everything to help, but there was no help for what was wrong.

"Then promise you'll keep in close touch with me."

"Haven't I always?"

"Not always," Akis reminded him.

No. The Friday night he'd read Zoe's good-bye letter, everything had become a blur until Akis had found him on Sunday morning. By now he'd gotten the message that she had no regrets over leaving him. None.

While he'd waited in the hope that he'd hear from her, he'd gone through every phase of pain and agony. Maybe it would never leave him. Desperate for some relief, he flew to Paxos. When the helicopter dropped him off, he got in his car. After buying some roses in town, he headed for their family church on the summit.

A breeze came up this time of day, filling the air with the scent of vanilla from the yellow broom growing on the hillsides. He pulled off the road and got out. The cemetery was around the back. Sixteen years ago he and Akis had buried their father next to their mother. They'd been young and their grief had been exquisite. In their need they'd clung to each other.

Vasso walked around and placed the tub of roses in front of the headstone. Then he put a knee down and read what was inscribed on the stone until it became a blur. As if it had been yesterday, he still remembered a conversation they'd had with their father before he'd died.

"You're only in your teens and you'll meet a lot of women before you're grown up. When you find *the* one, you must treat her like a queen. Your mother was my queen. I cherished and respected her from the beginning. She deserved that because not only was she going to be my wife, she was going to be the mother of our children."

Tears dripped off Vasso's chin.

"I've found my queen, *Papa,* but her fear of dying early of the same disease as you has made it impossible for us to be together.

I don't know how you handled it when our mother died, but somehow you lived through the grief. If you could do it, so can I. I'm the big brother. I *have* to.

"Wouldn't you know Akis is doing much better than I am because he's found the love of his life? They're going to have a baby." His shoulders heaved. "I'm so happy for them. I want to be happy, too. But the real truth of it is… I *have* to find a way for that to happen, *Papa,* otherwise this life no longer makes sense."

Vasso stayed there until he heard the voices of children playing on the slope below him. That meant school was out for the day. He'd been here long enough and wiped the tears with the side of his arm. It was time to drive back to the house and take stock of what he was going to do with his life from here on out.

Something had to change. To go on mourning for something that wasn't meant to be was destructive. He had a business to run. One day soon he'd be an uncle to his brother's child. Vasso intended to love him or her and give all the support he could.

After reaching the car, he drove home with

the windows open, taking the lower road that wound along the coastline. As he rounded a curve he saw a cyclist in the far distance. It was a beautiful day. Vasso didn't wonder that someone was out enjoying the sea air.

But when the helmeted figure suddenly disappeared from sight, Vasso was surprised. There was only one turnoff along this particular stretch of road. It led to his beach house. Curious to know if he had a visitor, or if the cyclist was simply a tourist out sightseeing, he stepped on the gas.

When he reached the turnoff, he came close to having a heart attack. Despite the helmet, Vasso could never mistake that well-endowed figure or those shapely legs headed for his house.

It was Zoe on the bike!

He stayed a few yards behind and watched the beautiful sight in front of him, trying to absorb the fact that she was back on the island.

The way she was pedaling, he could tell she was tired. At some point she must have sensed someone was behind her. When she looked over her right shoulder, she let out a cry and lost control of the bike. In the next second it fell over, taking her with it.

Terrified she could be hurt, Vasso stopped on a dime and jumped out of the car. But she'd recovered before he could reach her and was on her feet. His eyes were drawn to the English printed in blue on her white T-shirt with the high V-neck. *I'd rather be in Greece.*

If this was a private message to him, he was receiving it loud and clear. The way she filled it out caused him to tremble.

"Zoe—I'm so sorry. Are you hurt?"

Those shimmering green eyes fastened on him. "Heavens, no. I'm such a klutz."

She looked so adorable in that helmet and those shorts, he could hardly find his voice. "Of course you're not. I should have called out or honked so you'd know I was behind you. But to be honest, I thought maybe I was hallucinating to see you in front of me."

He watched her get back on the bike. "I was coming to visit you."

His heart pounded like thunder. "This has to be perfect timing because I haven't been here for several weeks."

"I probably should have phoned you, but

after I got off the ferry earlier, I just decided to come and take my chances." She flashed him one of those brilliant smiles that melted his insides. "Beat you to the house!"

He had a hundred questions to ask, but whatever the reason that had brought Zoe back to Paxos, he didn't care. It was enough to see her again. Something was very different. Her whole body seemed to sparkle with life.

She rode toward the house with more vigor than before, convincing him she hadn't hurt herself. He got back in his car and drove slowly the rest of the way. Zoe reached their destination first and put on the kickstand. She was waiting for him as he parked his car and got out.

"Where are you staying?"

"I don't know yet. Kyria Panos let me leave my luggage with her."

His mind was reeling. "You must be thirsty. Come in the house and we'll both have a soda."

Another smile from her turned his insides to butter. "You're a lifesaver."

They walked to the back door. Using his remote to let them in the house, he said, "The guest bathroom is behind that door at the far end of the kitchen."

"Thanks. I'm a mess."

The most gorgeous mess he'd ever seen. While she disappeared, he took the stairs two at a time to the loft and changed into shorts and a T-shirt. Before she came out, he hurried down to the kitchen in sandals and produced some colas from the fridge for them.

When she emerged she was *sans* the helmet. Her blond hair was attractively disheveled. Vasso wanted to plunge his fingers into it and kiss the very life out of her. Her flushed skin, in fact every single thing about her, was too desirable. But he'd learned a terrible lesson since the day she'd left Greece. He'd pushed her too hard, too soon, and wouldn't be making that mistake again.

He handed her a drink. "Welcome back to Greece." He clicked his can against hers and swallowed half the contents in one long gulp. "I like your T-shirt."

"The second I saw it, I had to have it and bought it from Kyria Panos earlier. She let me change shirts in her bathroom."

"You've made a friend there."

She sipped her drink. "Everyone is a friend

on this island. Gus waved to me from the bus while I was riding on the road to your house."

"I take it you haven't seen Yiannis yet."

"No. If I couldn't find you, I was planning to bike to the center."

"You look wonderful in those shorts, Zoe."

She blushed. "Thank you."

"I'm used to seeing you in skirts and dresses."

"I know. They make a nice change. You look wonderful, too."

He didn't know how long he could resist crushing her in his arms, but he needed answers. "Shall we go out on the deck?"

"I'd love it."

They walked over to the sliding doors. She sat on one of the loungers while he pulled a chair around next to her. "Tell me what happened when you went back to New York."

He listened as she gave him an account. They were both circling the giant elephant standing on the deck, but he needed to let her guide this conversation if he wanted to know the reason she'd come back. If she was only here for a few days, he couldn't bear it.

"While I was there, I had to go in for my six-weeks checkup."

This was too much. Vasso broke out in a cold sweat and got up, too restless to sit still. He turned on his heel. "Were you given a death sentence and a date? Is that why you're here? To thank me one more time and say a final goodbye?"

"Vasso—" She paled and shot to her feet.

"Because if you are, I could have done without this visit. You know damn well why I asked you to marry me. Can you possibly understand the pain you've inflicted by turning up here now?" The words had gushed out. He couldn't take them back.

"Do you want to hear the exact quote I got from my doctor?"

"Actually I don't." She seemed determined to tell him, but he couldn't go through this agony again and started for the doorway into the house.

She followed him. "He said, 'There's no recurrence of cancer, Zoe. I'm giving you another clean bill of health. In people like you with none of the other complicating factors, it's possible you'll live a full life.'"

Vasso wheeled around. "But you still don't believe him."

"You didn't let me finish. I told him about you and me."

He closed his eyes tightly. "Go on."

"The doctor said, 'You're a damn fool if you don't fly back there and tell him yes. I don't want to see you in my office again unless you have a wedding ring on your finger'!" Zoe moved closer to him.

"Little did he know he was speaking to the converted. After being the recipient of a miracle, I realized I would be an ungrateful wretch if I didn't embrace life fully. He reminded me that we are all facing a death sentence in life, but most of us don't have a time frame.

"Vasso—I came back because I want to spend the rest of my life with you. You have to know I love you to the depths of my being. I want to have children with you. I want the privilege of being called Kyria Giannopoulos, the wife who has a husband like no other in existence.

"You have no idea how handsome and spectacular you are. I lost my breath the first time I laid eyes on you, and I've never completely recovered. You're probably going to think I'm crazy, but I'm thankful I came down with the disease. It brought me to you. If you'll ask me again to marry you, I promise to make you happy because I'm the happiest woman alive to be loved by you."

He could feel the ice melting around his heart. "So you don't think I want you to be my wife because I feel responsible for you?"

"No, darling. I only said that because I was so afraid you couldn't love me the way I loved you. I know you're not perfect, but you are to me," her voice trembled.

"Then come here to me and show me."

She flew into his arms. When he felt them wind around his neck, he carried her in the house and followed her down on the couch. *"Agape mou...* I'm so in love with you I thought I was going to die when I read your letter.

"You're the woman my father was talking about. You're *the* one. I knew it when you walked in the center's office bringing spring with you. I'll never forget that moment. The fierce beating of my heart almost broke my rib cage. You're so sweet and so funny and so fun and so endearing and so beautiful and so kind and so compassionate all at the same time. I love you," he cried. *"I love you, Zoe."*

He broke off telling her all the things she meant to him because her mouth got in the way. That luscious mouth that thrilled him in ways he'd never even dreamed possible. They couldn't get enough of each other. Her body melted against him. Their legs entwined and they forgot everything except the joy of loving each other at last.

If it hadn't been for his phone ringing, he didn't know when they would have surfaced. He let it ring because he had to do something else first.

"Maybe you should get that. It could be important," she whispered against his jaw.

"I'm pretty sure it's Akis calling to find out if I'm all right."

A frown marred her lovely features. "He loves you so much."

"I almost lost it when I read your letter. Akis found me here two days later. Just so he won't worry and come flying over here to find out if I'm still alive, just answer me one question, then I'll listen to the message. Will you marry me, Thespinis Zachos? We've already been through the sickness and health part. Will you be my love through life? I adore you."

Her eyes glistened with tears. "You already know my answer. I have a secret. The morning I got off the plane and found you waiting to pick me up at the airport, I wanted to be your wife. I couldn't imagine anything more wonderful." She buried her face in his neck. "You just don't know how much I love you."

He gave her another fierce kiss before getting up to find his phone on the table. "It's from my brother."

"Call him so he won't worry. I'll wait right here for you."

Without listening to the message, he called him back.

"Thanks for returning my call, bro."

"I'm glad you phoned. How would you like to be the best man at my wedding?"

"What?"

"She's back and we're getting married as soon as we can."

Akis let out a sound of pure joy then shouted the news to Raina who was in the background and gave her own happy cry. "Tell that Zoe I love her already."

Vasso stared down at her. "I will. She's easy to love."

"I only have one piece of advice. Remember what *Papa* said."

He knew. Treat Zoe like a queen. "I remember."

"Come on over for dinner so we can celebrate."

"You mean now?"

"Now! And you know why." Vasso knew exactly why. "We're expecting you." Akis clicked off.

Vasso hung up and leaned over Zoe. "We're invited for dinner."

"I don't want to move, but considering it's your brother…." She sat up and kissed him passionately. "You two have been through everything together. I get it."

He knew she did. "We'll go in the cruiser. I'll phone Kyria Panos and tell her we'll be by for your luggage later tonight."

CHAPTER TEN

October 16, Paxos Island

"Iris!" Zoe cried out when she saw Akis help her old friend from New York out of the helicopter that had landed on the center's roof. She ran to her and they clung. "This is the best present I could have. You've been like a mother to me. I'm just so thankful you could come for the wedding."

"I wouldn't have missed it. Neither would Father Debakis."

Zoe's eyes lit on the priest who was getting out of the helicopter. The two of them had flown over yesterday and had stayed at the penthouse.

She left Iris long enough to run to the great man she owed her life to. "Oh, Father—I'm so glad you could come to marry us."

He hugged her hard. "It's my privilege. I had a feeling about the two of you a long time ago."

"Nothing gets past you."

Akis walked over to them. "Come on, everyone. Let's get on the elevator. Raina is waiting to help you into your wedding dress. Yiannis will drive you and Raina to the church. I'll drive everyone else in my car.

"Needless to say my older brother is climbing the walls waiting for the ceremony to begin. For his sake, I beg you to hurry, Zoe."

The best man's comment produced laughter from everyone and brought roses to Zoe's cheeks. She had to pinch herself that this was real and that she was getting married to Vasso.

When they reached the main floor, Zoe hurried along the hall to a private room where Raina was waiting.

"They've arrived!"

"Thank heaven! I've had three phone calls from Vasso. If he doesn't see you soon, he's going to have a nervous breakdown."

"Well we can't have that."

Zoe got out of her skirt and blouse and stepped into the white floor-length wedding dress. Raina had dared her to wear the latest fashion. It was strapless, something she would never have picked out on her own. But Raina insisted she was a knockout in it. This was one time she needed to render her soon-to-be husband *speechless*.

"Oh, Raina. It's so fun having you to help me. What I would have given for a sister like you."

"I feel the same way. Today I'm getting her. We're the luckiest women in the world."

"Yup. In a little while I'll be married to a god, too."

"They really are," Raina murmured. "But you've still got your perfect figure while I'm beginning to get a bump."

"If you ever saw the way Akis looks at you when you're not aware of it, you'd know you and the baby are his whole world."

"Today the focus is on you. I have something for you, Zoe. Vasso asked me to give this to you."

With trembling hands, Zoe opened the satin-lined jewelry box. Inside lay a strand of gleaming pearls. A card sat on top. "*For my queen.*"

She looked at Raina in puzzlement. "He thinks of me as his queen?"

Raina nodded. "Akis gave me the same kind of pearls with the same sentiment on his card. When I asked him about it, he told me that his father had told them the women they would choose would be their queens and they needed to treat them like one."

"What a fabulous father he was. Vasso has always treated me like that."

"So has Akis. Now hold still while I put this around your neck."

Zoe's emotions were spilling out all over to feel the pearls against her skin. She'd already done her hair and applied her makeup. She wore pearl studs in her ears.

"Now for the crowning glory." Raina walked over and put the shoulder-length lace mantilla over her head. "When you get to the church, pull it over your face. You know? I think I'd better have an ambulance standing by. After Vasso sees you, anything could happen."

"You're such a tease."

"I'm only speaking the truth." She turned and opened a long florist's box. Inside was a sheaf of flowers. Raina laid it in the crook of Zoe's arm.

"Aren't they lovely!" Her eyes took in the all-white arrangement: white roses, cymbidium orchids, hydrangeas and stephanotises. "My mother would have planned a bouquet just like this for me. She loved white flowers."

"Don't we all." They both breathed in the heavenly scent.

Zoe eyed her dearest new friend. "You look absolutely stunning in that blue silk suit." Raina wore a gardenia in the lapel.

"Except that I had to undo the zipper to get into it. I think I can get away with it for as long as we're at the church." She smiled at Zoe. "Ready?"

"Yes," she said emotionally.

They left the room and headed for the main entrance. When they walked outside by the fountain Zoe saw Yianni. He looked splendid wearing his former naval uniform. "You're a sight for sore eyes, Zoe."

"So are you. I can see why your wife grabbed you up the second she met you."

"You look radiant today." He kissed her

forehead then pulled the edge of the veil down to cover her face.

"Thank you for standing in for my father."

"It's an honor. Now let's get you in the car and be off. Your fiancé is waiting for you. I've had two phone calls from Vasso. He's going to have a coronary if we don't arrive soon."

Zoe laughed and got in the rear of the limo. Raina helped her with her dress. Yianni checked to make sure everything was secure then he drove them through the olive groves and up the steep hillside to the glistening white church at the summit. It made an imposing sight overlooking the sea.

This was the church where Raina and Akis had been married by his family priest. Their parents had been buried in the cemetery behind it. This was the place where history had been made and was still being made today by another Giannopoulos son.

Father Debakis would be doing the honors with the other priest's help. This was right out of a fairy tale.

The closer they got, she could see dozens of cars lining both sides of the road leading to the church. Akis and his best friend Theo had taken care of the invitations. Zoe feared there wouldn't be enough room in the church to accommodate everyone.

Vasso had told her not to worry. The priest would leave the front doors open and set up chairs for those people who couldn't get inside. A real Greek wedding was a high point no one wanted to miss.

When they came around the bend she could see dozens of beautifully dressed guests seated at tables outside with white ribbons on the chairs. But that wasn't all. Behind the chairs were throngs of people willing to stand.

Raina and Theo's wife Chloe had made the arrangements for the food, which would be served on the grounds after the ceremony, followed by singing and dancing. She promised they wouldn't run out of food, but when Zoe saw the amount of people congregated, it shocked her.

Yianni drove past the cars and circled around to the front steps of the church. Suddenly all Zoe could see was Vasso. He stood at the open doors waiting for her in a formal midnight-blue suit with a white rose in the lapel. She couldn't hold back her cry when she saw him. No man was ever created like him.

Once the limo came to a stop, he walked toward her with a loving look in his black eyes that lit up her whole body. Yianni came around the door to help her out. But it was Vasso who grasped her hand and squeezed it.

Raina took the flowers from her and walked behind them with Yianni while Vasso led her into the church. She'd been in here several times in the last few weeks and thought it an exquisite jewel. The smell of incense and flowers greeted them as they moved toward Father Debakis, decked out in his priestly finery. The interior was so full people who hadn't found a seat were lined up against the walls.

Both she and Vasso wanted a traditional wedding to honor their parents. Her heart pounded so hard she knew he could feel its beat through her hand. When they arrived at the altar, he leaned over and lifted the veil. The love pouring from his soul was evident in those gorgeous black eyes.

If ever there was a time to faint, it was now. But she didn't feel light-headed. She felt a spirit of joy wash over her as they grasped hands and entered into this sacred ritual that would make him her husband.

They went through the different stages of the ring ceremony until it came to the union of the bride and groom with the crowning. This was the part she'd been looking forward to. The priest took two crowns with ribbons from the altar table, blessed them, then put the crowns on their heads.

"Oh, Lord our God, crown them with glory and honor."

The other priest exchanged their crowns over their heads to seal the union. He read from the Gospel account of the wedding in Cana. After a prayer, he passed the common cup for them to take a sip of the wine. This was the part that meant they shared equally in the process of life. Father Debakis then led them around the table three times.

This was where her heart beat wildly as the two of them stared at each other while they made circles. A hint of a smile broke the corners of Vasso's mouth. Zoe felt this part of the wedding ceremony was terribly romantic, but she'd never admit it to anyone but him. He looked so handsome with the crown on she wanted a picture of him just like that.

When they faced the priest again, he removed their crowns. His eyes rested kindly on Vasso. "Be magnified, O Bridegroom, as Abraham." Then he looked at Zoe with such tenderness she was deeply moved. "And you, O Bride, be magnified as was Sarah, and live a long, fruitful life."

He'd added those words meant just for her. Once again she was overcome with gratitude that out of the shadows, she'd emerged into a light greater than the one she could see with the naked eye.

Father Debakis placed a Bible in both their hands and said a final prayer. He smiled at them. "Congratulations, Kyrie and Kyria Giannopoulos. Just think, Vasso," he whispered. "If I hadn't called you…"

"I don't want to think about it, Father," he whispered back. He put his arm around Zoe's waist and they faced the congregation. She'd never seen so many smiling faces in her life, but one stood out above the rest.

It was Akis. He and Vasso exchanged a silent message that was so sweet and said so much Zoe could hardly breathe with the love she could see between the two of them.

Suddenly Vasso lowered his mouth to her ear. "Let the fun begin."

Raina came forward to hand her the sheaf of flowers. After she stepped away, Zoe and Vasso started walking down the aisle. Everyone was here. Olympia and Nestor had come from the center. She smiled at Kyria Lasko, Kyria Panos, Gus the bus driver, Iris, and her doctor from the center in Astoria.

With each step, people said Vasso's name; they were the managers from some of their stores, family friends, their mutual friends, two of the helicopter pilots, the woman called Elpis who'd given the boys free sweets when they were young. The list went on and on. When they reached the rear of the church and stepped outside, there was cheering and music. People rushed to congratulate them.

The paparazzi were out in full measure, but Zoe didn't care. She was too happy to be married to her heart's desire to have a care in the world. They had their own videographer there to record the proceedings of the day.

"Give us a kiss with your husband, Kyria Giannopoulos."

"Gladly!" She turned to Vasso. There was

a wild look in his eye before he caught her to him and kissed the life out of her in front of everyone. They were a little drunk with happiness. The taste of his mouth was sweeter than any wine. She would never be able to get enough of it. Anyone could see that.

Part of her felt a fierce pride at the turn-out. If she had a megaphone and dared, she'd love to say, "Look at these poor Giannopoulos boys now! Eat your hearts out!" But of course she couldn't say or do that.

The caterers had arrived and had set up more tables to accommodate the huge crowd. With the musicians in place, the dancing began. Yianni grabbed Zoe's other hand and several dozen people joined to form a line. They danced through the tables while everyone threw rice. The excitement had made her heady.

Every time Vasso's fiery eyes met hers, her heart palpitated right out of her chest. She knew what he was thinking. It was all she could think about. Their wedding night.

Zoe had been waiting all her life for the time when she would marry. She actually wanted to call Ms. Kallistos one day and tell her that *she* was the person responsible for the miracle that had come into Zoe's life. But on reflection it wouldn't be a good idea.

Vasso had hired Alexandra and there was no doubt in Zoe's mind the manager had been crazy about him from day one. Through Akis she'd learned that Sofia Peri had left her husband and wanted Vasso back. Zoe couldn't blame her for that. Today she could feel sorry for every woman alive who wasn't married to her Apollo.

Today she'd met so many people who thought the world of Vasso and Akis. If their father were still alive, he would be so proud of them. *And their mother...* Zoe had seen the few pictures they had of her. She'd been a beauty. That's why the two brothers were so gorgeous.

Oh, Vasso. I can't wait until we're alone. Really alone.

The party went on several hours. Toasts were made to the happy couple. As Zoe danced with Akis, Vasso danced with Raina. Then she saw the brothers signal each other. The next thing she knew Akis whirled her toward the limousine where Yianni was parked in front of the church.

Akis opened the rear door and hurried her inside. Vasso came around the other side and slid in next to her. The second his door closed, the limo started moving. Everyone saw them leave and gave out shouts. But Zoe was caught in Vasso's arms. His mouth came down on hers and the world whirled away. When he lifted his lips, she realized the car had come to a stop outside Vasso's beach house.

He opened the door and stepped out. Then he helped her. The second she was on her feet he picked her up and carried her in his arms. "Thank you, Yiannis."

The car drove off, leaving them alone. "I've been dreaming about doing this for weeks, Zoe."

"So have I, darling."

Vasso unlocked the back door with the remote and carried her over the threshold. He didn't stop until he'd gained the loft. "I've never been up here before," she said as he twirled her around.

"That was the plan. Thank heaven the long wait is finally over."

"I love you, my darling Vasso. *I love you.*"

* * *

After they'd made love throughout the night, Vasso's beautiful wife fell asleep around five o'clock, but he was still wide awake. Adrenaline rushed through his system like a never-ending fire.

Her wedding dress lay over one of the chairs, her mantilla on the dresser with her wedding flowers. Their scent filled the loft. He'd thrown his wedding suit over another chair. The white rose was still in the lapel.

She was the most unselfish lover he could ever have imagined. For the next little while he lay on his side holding her loosely in his arms so he could study her beautiful features. He still couldn't believe she was his wife, all signed, sealed and delivered to be his, now and forever.

Her mouth was like a half-opened rose, lush with a red tint, like a strawberry. He needed to taste her again and again and never stop. As soon as he started to kiss her in earnest, she made a little moan and her eyes opened.

"Vasso—I dreamed I was kissing you, but I really *am* kissing you."

He laughed deep in his throat. "I wanted

to kiss you good morning. It wasn't nice of me to wake you up, but I'm so in love with you, I don't think I'll ever be able to leave you alone."

"Please don't, or I won't be able to bear it." She rolled over and kissed him so deeply that age-old ritual started again. They didn't come up for breath for several more hours.

Vasso finally lifted his mouth from hers. "Did I tell you yet how gorgeous you looked in that wedding dress? I could hardly breathe when you got out of the limo."

"Raina said I should wear it to give you a jolt."

"You did a lot more than that. Every man at the wedding would have given anything to be in my place. She has the right instincts. Raina's so good for Akis."

"I love her already."

"So do I."

"You kind of stopped traffic yourself. Have I told you yet how good you are for me? You make me thankful to have been born a woman. Seriously, Vasso, I'm so wild about you I think maybe there's something wrong with me."

"I'll never complain." He kissed every feature. "So you don't mind that I'm invading your space?"

"I must have been crazy when I said that."

"It's because you never lived with a man and didn't know it's the only way for a man and woman to experience true joy. These last few years I knew that the most important element in my life was missing. But not anymore." He crushed her body to his, kissing her neck and throat. "Where do you want to go on our honeymoon?"

"Right here with you."

"We could go anywhere," he murmured against her lips.

"I know. What do you say we wait to take a trip after we find out we're going to have a baby."

Vasso smoothed the hair off her forehead. "You want a baby soon?"

"You know I do. I'm so envious of Raina and Akis. There's no reason to wait. You heard what Father Debakis said. Be fruitful."

He rolled her over and looked deep into her eyes. "Maybe he already knows something we don't."

"I know. Exciting, isn't it?"

"In that case we'll just stay here until we get it right."

She cupped his face and pulled him down to press a passionate kiss to his mouth. "I was hoping you'd say that. If you think I'm shameful, I don't care. I need you with every particle of my being."

His expression sobered. He kissed her hands and moved them to either side of her head. "Don't you know you've made me whole? A thrill went through me when you circled the altar with me. I felt your love binding me tighter and tighter."

"I had that same wonderful feeling," she cried softly. "Our ceremony was holy, but it was also very romantic."

He smiled. "Only you could come up with the perfect description. That's because there's only one perfect you. You're the light of my life, *agape mou*. Kiss me again, Kyria Giannopoulos."

Three hours later he heard his cell vibrate. Only one person would be texting him.

Zoe smiled. "That has to be your brother. I love how close you are. Put him out of his misery and tell him we're deliriously happy."

Vasso reached for the phone on the bedside table. "He says to turn on the news. Do you want to watch?"

"No. I don't need to see my beloved husband on TV when I've got him right here in my arms."

"That's just another one of the thousand reasons I love you more than life itself." He buried his face in her neck, crying her name over and over again.

* * * * *

COMING NEXT MONTH FROM

HARLEQUIN

Romance

Available October 6, 2015

#4491 SOLDIER, HERO...HUSBAND?
The Vineyards of Calanetti
by Cara Colter

Since becoming a widow, Isabella Rossi has been sleepwalking through life. But when she meets former navy SEAL Connor, his delicious kisses are waking her up! Connor can't forget his past, but Isabella is determined to fight for the future they both deserve...

#4492 FALLING FOR MR. DECEMBER
by Kate Hardy

Photographer Sammy's never dreamed of forever, but sparks fly when she meets gorgeous barrister Nick Kennedy. As she gets to know the man behind the pinstripes, dare she hope Nick will make it a Christmas to remember with the most magical gift of all—his heart?

#4493 THE BABY WHO SAVED CHRISTMAS
by Alison Roberts

Brooding celebrity chef Julien is guardian of his tiny orphaned nephew... and completely out of his depth! Alice Macmillan's arrival is the answer to his prayers, and as snowflakes start falling, could this Christmas see the beginning of their own fledgling family?

#4494 A PROPOSAL WORTH MILLIONS
by Sophie Pembroke

Focused on making her business a success, Sadie Sullivan doesn't need any distractions. But when her secret crush—Dylan—arrives with an irresistible proposal, the chemistry she's long tried to ignore suddenly feels very real... As Sadie signs along the dotted line, it seems this deal might just lead to sun, sea and a happily-ever-after!

**YOU CAN FIND MORE INFORMATION
ON UPCOMING HARLEQUIN® TITLES,
FREE EXCERPTS AND MORE AT
WWW.HARLEQUIN.COM.**

HRLPCNM0915

LARGER-PRINT BOOKS!

GET 2 FREE LARGER-PRINT NOVELS PLUS
2 FREE GIFTS!

HARLEQUIN®

Romance

From the Heart, For the Heart

YES! Please send me 2 FREE LARGER-PRINT Harlequin® Romance novels and my 2 FREE gifts (gifts are worth about $10). After receiving them, if I don't wish to receive any more books, I can return the shipping statement marked "cancel." If I don't cancel, I will receive 4 brand-new novels every month and be billed just $5.09 per book in the U.S. or $5.49 per book in Canada. That's a savings of at least 15% off the cover price! It's quite a bargain! Shipping and handling is just 50¢ per book in the U.S. and 75¢ per book in Canada.* I understand that accepting the 2 free books and gifts places me under no obligation to buy anything. I can always return a shipment and cancel at any time. Even if I never buy another book, the two free books and gifts are mine to keep forever.

119/319 HDN GHWC

Name _____ (PLEASE PRINT)

Address _____ Apt. #

City _____ State/Prov. _____ Zip/Postal Code

Signature (if under 18, a parent or guardian must sign)

Mail to the **Reader Service:**
IN U.S.A.: P.O. Box 1867, Buffalo, NY 14240-1867
IN CANADA: P.O. Box 609, Fort Erie, Ontario L2A 5X3
Want to try two free books from another line?
Call 1-800-873-8635 or visit www.ReaderService.com.

* Terms and prices subject to change without notice. Prices do not include applicable taxes. Sales tax applicable in N.Y. Canadian residents will be charged applicable taxes. Offer not valid in Quebec. This offer is limited to one order per household. Not valid for current subscribers to Harlequin Romance Larger-Print books. All orders subject to credit approval. Credit or debit balances in a customer's account(s) may be offset by any other outstanding balance owed by or to the customer. Please allow 4 to 6 weeks for delivery. Offer available while quantities last.

Your Privacy—The Reader Service is committed to protecting your privacy. Our Privacy Policy is available online at www.ReaderService.com or upon request from the Reader Service.

We make a portion of our mailing list available to reputable third parties that offer products we believe may interest you. If you prefer that we not exchange your name with third parties, or if you wish to clarify or modify your communication preferences, please visit us at www.ReaderService.com/consumerschoice or write to us at Reader Service Preference Service, P.O. Box 9062, Buffalo, NY 14240-9062. Include your complete name and address.

HRLP15

Nick Kennedy was spectacular, Sammy thought. Broad
shoulders, beautiful biceps, enough hair on his chest to
be sexy without him looking like a total gorilla, and a
definite six-pack.

Mr. December was going to be the best page on the calendar. He could probably sell the calendar all by himself.

"What?" he asked, clearly noting that she was staring
at him.

"Nothing," she said, embarrassed to discover that her
voice was slightly croaky. She really had to get a grip.
The last thing she needed was Nick to work out that she
was attracted to him. And he was bright. Scratch bright:
that kind of legal background meant he had to be super-
bright. So he'd be able to work it out quickly.

She got him to do a few more poses, moving around
and taking some shots from the side and some others
from the back. And, oh, his back was beautiful. She'd

love to do some proper nude studies of him. In a wood, looking for all the world like a statue of a Greek god.

Not that he'd agree to it. Not in a million years.

But a girl could dream…

"Okay. That's a wrap. You can get dressed now," she said. "And by the time I've loaded everything onto my laptop we'll be ready to go to dinner."

Once she'd finished downloading the pictures, she saved the files. "Is it okay for me to turn around now?" she asked with her back still toward Nick.

"Sure."

Rather than putting on the ratty T-shirt and tracksuit bottoms again, he was wearing the white tunic shirt— without the collar—the waistcoat and his court trousers.

Sammy's heart skipped a beat. Right now, with his formal dress very slightly disheveled, he looked as sexy as hell. If his hair was ever so slightly longer and someone had ruffled her hand through it to suggest that he'd just been thoroughly kissed, he'd look spectacular. In fact, he'd go straight to number one on the Sexiest Man in the World list. She itched to get her camera out again. And this time she'd make him pose very differently.

"Okay?" he asked.

No. Not okay at all.

Don't miss Kate Hardy's festive story
FALLING FOR MR DECEMBER,
available October 2015 wherever
Harlequin® Romance books and ebooks are sold.

www.Harlequin.com